Yorks[...]
Sh[...]

Edited by
Joan Thornton

Yorkshire Art Circus
1990

Published by Yorkshire Art Circus
School Lane, Glasshoughton, Castleford
West Yorkshire WF10 4QH
Telephone (0977) 550401

ISBN 0 947780 62 9
Classification: Fiction

Typesetting and printing by FM Repro Ltd.
Repro House, 69 Lumb Lane, Roberttown, Liversedge
West Yorkshire WF15 7NB

Yorkshire Art Circus is a unique book publisher. We link our books
with performances and exhibitions and offer workshops for the
first time writer.

Yorkshire Art Circus projects have successfully toured community
centres, colleges, galleries, clubs, galas and art centres. In all our
work we bring new artists to new audiences.

For details of our programme of performances, exhibitions, conferences and workshops, send for our brochure and book list at
the address above.

Yorkshire Art Circus is a non-profitmaking limited company.

Acknowledgements

Olive Fowler
Rachel Van Riel
Rachel Adam
Brian Lewis
Michael Yates

**We would like to thank the following organisations for sup-
port towards this book:**

Introduction

There was a time when anthologies of short stories were very popular. For the up-and-coming writer, they offered the good an opportunity to get between the covers with the great. Reputations were established in this way.

Now magazines and radio are the main outlets for short stories and although they have many advantages, and reach large audiences, a book is still more portable than a radio, more substantial than a magazine and more lasting than both. A book can give pleasure for years.

As a publisher, Yorkshire Art Circus specialises in books by Yorkshire writers. These books have usually been individual biographies or collected memories, anecdotes and photographs of specific communities. *Yorkshire Mixture* is Yorkshire Art Circus' first venture into fiction and aims to encourage talented creative writers, both established and new. Successful short story writing requires skills and structures very different from those found in novels, biographies and reminiscences.

In putting together this collection, hundreds of short stories have been received, read and enjoyed. It is intended that *Yorkshire Mixture* will become an annual anthology. Perhaps with this and future volumes we can help stem the decline of the short story anthology and bring new writing to appreciative readers.

Contents

Local Difficulties

Robert Jordan

I'll be glad when he's back on his feet, I can tell you. I don't mind helping, but it's not as though I were a relative or anything. I mean, it wouldn't be so bad if that brother-in-law of his could get round a bit more often. As things stand, it looks as though I'm going to be lumbered for quite some time to come.

I suppose it's expected of me, being his next door neighbour. But I've already got enough on my plate as it is, what with the bazaar coming up as well. There's a part of me wishes I'd never seen him lying there, or that I could have got somebody else to send for help, but there you are — just my luck.

All the same, when it comes down to it, he's nobody to blame but himself. I don't know how many times I'd told him. 'Mr Renshaw,' I used to say, 'You'll be coming a cropper one of these days. You're too old for that game. Let me send Harry round next Tuesday after he's done mine.' But would he listen? No, not him.

'It costs money,' he'd say, 'I'd rather do my own.' And off he'd go up the ladder, water spilling everywhere, trying to pull himself up with one hand, hauling the bucket up with the other. Should have been in a bloody circus, I always said.

Then he'd get to the top; pant, pant, pant, splash, splash, splash. 'See? What do I want with a window cleaner, eh?' Pulls the leather out of the bucket, slaps it up against the pane; water everywhere. Two minutes' worth of huffing and puffing, then it's back down the ladder again because he's no blessed water left.

Stone me, I used to think, all this for the sake of a couple of quid; not right upstairs if you ask me.

Anyway that's how he used to carry on and look where it got him — flat on his back. Lucky he didn't kill himself. I'll never forget the noise he made when he fell off that ladder. I was in the kitchen when I hears this crash, so I looks up and what do I see if it's not that stupid ladder of his slicing through the privet? Thanks, I thought, thanks a lot.

Then he starts with his 'Oh oh oh.' I thought, I'll give you some 'Oh oh oh' in a minute, my lad. So I rush outside and there he is sprawled on his back, blooming great beer gut heaving up and down, 'Oh oh oh — I can't move. I think I've broken my back.'

'You're lucky,' I said, which he was when you come to think of it, 'you could have killed yourself. Where did you fall from anyway?'

'Doctor,' he moans.

'You weren't right at the top, were you?'

'Doctor. Get me a doctor — please.'

Well, I could see he wasn't going to make any sense as he was, so I phoned for a doctor. He arrives, takes one look at him and decides to call an ambulance.

'He's had a bad fall,' says the doctor.

'He's lucky,' I says.

Well, the upshot of it is that he goes into hospital. They keep him in for God knows how long doing one test after another — tests for this, tests for that. At the end of it, they decide it's his back. I ask you, all these blessed tests just to find that out. I could have told them that. Well, it turns out he will be able to walk again on account of its not being broken. But he's not going to be able to do much for himself for some time since he can't support himself to get about and what have you.

Anyway, they say they can't do any more for him in hospital and that he's best off at home. Now that's all very well, but there's nobody to look after him at home. He's only got one relative living round here — that's his brother-in-law Jack — and he's busy most of the day. In the end, it's either me or nobody.

I could have well done without the bother but the doctor seemed to think that with me being the most frequent visitor, and being his next door neighbour, I'm the logical choice. Logical! It'd have been more logical to pay for a proper window cleaner in the first place but . . . well, there you go.

So here he is back at home, and here I am fetching and carrying for him, cooking his meals and generally clearing up after him. I couldn't believe it when I first saw the state that house was in. I don't know what he reckons to do for food. All I could find in the house were three tins of mushroom soup, a tin of peaches and a piece of cheese that could have walked to the dustbin by itself. Anyway, I did some soup for him, then I took him up the peaches.

'I don't like peaches,' he says. 'They don't agree with me.'

'Then why buy them?' I said.

'They're for in case anybody dops in.'

Strewth!

And you should have seen the mess: clothes everywhere, pots not washed, bath black bright. I started tidying up and doing, and I hear this voice from the bedroom.

'What are you up to, Mrs Armitage?'

'I'm just putting these clothes away.'

'Don't do that. I shan't know where anything is.'

I said: 'There's clothes everywhere, Mr Renshaw. It's like a jumble sale.'

'But they're all sorted,' he says, 'I know just where I can put my hands on them.'

And I'm thinking — yes, and I know where I could put my hands on you.

To cap it all, as soon as I'd finished fussing around after him, I had a meeting to go to — the bazaar. Every year it's the same. The vicar says, 'I think a bazaar would be just the thing to swell the church funds,' and Eva Tyson swings into action.

God help us! My Jim used to organise that bazaar — right down to the last detail. Everybody knew exactly what they were doing. There was no fuss, no bother and no cockups. The year after he died, Eva Tyson took over and turned it into a right rigmarole. She runs everything, does nothing and we all flap about like headless chickens.

This year for some reason the church hall wasn't good enough for the meetings, so we all had to troop over to Eva's house.

'It'll be cosier there,' she said.

I thought, yes, and we'll all be expected to admire that lounge of yours that's just been redecorated.

We were supposed to be starting at seven but it was half past before everyone turned up. The vicar was last as usual. You should have seen the fuss she made over him when he finally arrived.

'Oh, Mr Howson, we're all so pleased you were able to come.'

If it had been anybody else, she'd have jumped down their throats for being late. Anyway, by the time we'd all been served with tea and cakes, it was quarter-to-eight.

'Firstly,' she said, 'I should like to welcome you all to our meeting tonight, the aim of which being to plan arrangements for the forthcoming church bazaar.'

Typical, I thought — can't string a few words together without making it sound as though she's unveiling a bloody monument.

'I'd like you all to take one of these.' Then she starts dishing out a sheaf of papers. 'That's right — take one and pass the rest on.'

Mine arrives, and I see at the top it says — 'CHURCH BAZAAR, Chief Duties and Responsibilities.'

'What's this in aid of?' I said.

'It's a list of chief duties and responsibilities for all those involved in the church bazaar.'

'But this is supposed to be a planning meeting,' I said. 'It looks as though you've already got everything cut and dried.'

'Forward planning, Mrs Armitage.'

Forward planning my backside, I thought, but I didn't say anything — I just looked at her.

'I must say,' chimes up the vicar, 'this is all very impressive Mrs Tyson. I see you've got me down to make the corn dollies.'

'Well, I know it's a hobby of yours, and I thought it would be in keeping with Mr Quigley's morris dancing display. After the dancing's finished, we could put the dollies up for sale.'

'That's a terrific idea,' says the vicar. 'Don't you agree, Mr Quigley?'

'Oh, yes, yes, I do.' He sounded as though he'd only just woken up.

'Do you get the drift now?' says Eva. 'Everybody is specifically responsible for something or other.'

'Yes,' I said, 'but you've got me down as tombola and cakes.'

'That's right. I thought you could sell the tickets, run the draw and make a few cakes to be given as the smaller prizes. You might like to make, say, a dozen cakes. Then the surplus can be put on sale along with the rest of the home produce.'

'But we don't have a drum,' I said. 'You need a drum to put the tickets in. If you remember, somebody suggested having a tombola last year and we had to abandon it because we didn't have a drum. We wound up tying all the tickets to balloons and awarding prizes for those that went farthest.'

'I remember,' says Mr Quigley. 'My ticket reached

Doncaster but I never got a prize. Right swizz, if you ask me.'

'Well there you are then,' says Eva, beaming. 'A tombola is a much better idea. You needn't worry about the drum — you can make one easily enough out of cardboard or something.'

All right for her to say that, I thought, but I'm supposed to be helping with a church bazaar, not presenting sodding Blue Peter.

'And you need have no concern about the big day: I shall be there to draw the winning tickets.'

I could just picture it — Eva Tyson there in a big hat and fur coat, looking like the Lady Mayoress. She'd be in her element.

'Anyway,' she says, 'I'll just run through the list, so we all know what's expected of us. There's Mrs Armitage on tombola and cakes, Mr Howson corn dollies, Mr Quigley morris dancing, Mrs Richardson on wines and jams, Mr and Mrs Stoker to organise second-hand clothes, books and records — your van will be handy for that won't it, Mr Stoker? And Mr Lever to rehearse the barbershop quartet — for which we still need volunteers, by the way. We can sort out other matters as and when they arise. Everybody in the picture?'

'What are you responsible for?' I said.

'Well, I'm in charge of the organisation and implementation of the whole thing.'

'Yes, I know, but isn't there anything specific you'll be doing?'

She thought for a few seconds, scrutinised the sheet, then announced: 'I, in addition, shall arrange the bunting.'

Well, I thought, we can all sleep easier tonight for knowing that.

I decided to call in to see Mr Renshaw on the way back. He'd got his brother-in-law with him. I'd only met him once before — at the hospital. He'd turned up straight from work, still had his apron on and smelled a bit of sour milk. This time though, he was dolled up to the nines: shiny shoes, brown check suit, camel-coloured coat with a felt collar, and a beige trilby which he lifted as soon as I went into the room.

'This is my brother-in-law, Jack,' says Mr Renshaw.

'I know. I met him at the hospital. How d'you do?'

'Enchanted,' he says.

Strewth, I thought, we've got a right one here — must be the clothes that bring it on.

I went next door to get some cocoa, made us all a cup, then went to see if Mr Renshaw wanted anything else before I went to bed.

'No,' he says, 'I dare say I'll last while breakfast.'

'Right then, I'll be off.' Then I notice a big cardboard box on top of the wardrobe. 'Do you mind if I have that — if you're not using it?'

'Suppose not. What do you want it for?'

So I have to explain all about the church bazaar and the drum for the tombola.

'Oh,' Jack pipes up. 'You needn't worry about that. I've got the very thing at home, I'll drop it off, next time I call.' I'm surprised at this, but I just say: 'Well, thanks very much, Mr Fletcher.'

'Not at all,' he says. 'It's a pleasure to be of assistance and please, do call me Jack.' And all the time his trilby's popping up and down like a lavatory seat.

'Thanks Jack.' Smooth beggar!

'I've managed to get Mr Renshaw's place sorted out a bit now. I've been out shopping for him and the house is a damn sight cleaner than it was. He's still as fussy as ever about his food, but I know I can always keep him quiet with mushroom soup.

Their Jack called today while I was round there. As soon as he saw me, he said, 'Just a minute I'll be right back. It's in the car.'

I'm thinking what the devil's he on about? Then I remember about the drum. Next thing, there's all this panting and wheezing and clattering and what have you. I look down the stairs and there he is — blooming great cylinder thing wedged between him and the wall.

'For God's sake Jack, whatever do you think you're up to? You'll be having a heart attack!' I mean, he's not that far off sixty, and there he is struggling with this enormous metal thing. 'Stay there,' I said, 'I'll come down to you. You'll do yourself a mischief if you try to bring it upstairs.'

I go down to him and he blurts out, 'Do you like it? You'll get a few raffle tickets in there, won't you?'

Well, I don't know what to say. It's a drum all right; and I see that he's made a frame to stand it on, and he's welded a handle to one end of it. But the daft thing is that it's made out of an old milk churn.

'It's made out of an old milk churn,' he says.

'So I see.'

'Had it for years. My father brought it home from somewhere or other. I knew it'd come in handy one day. What do you think?'

So I say the only thing I can. 'It's incredible.'

Then there we are. Both gawping at it on its stand, as though it's a baby in a cot. Eventually I ask, 'How do you get the tickets in and out?'

'What do you mean?'

'Well, usually there's a little door to open in the top. You know — so you can get at the tickets.'

'No problem,' he says, 'you just take the lid off the churn. See?' and he pulls it off.

'Oh, of course,' I say. 'It's different, anyway.'

'It's unique,' he says. So now we know.

I was glad to get the business of the tombola drum out of the way. Right, I thought, now it's just a matter of making a few cakes and flogging the tickets. I hadn't bargained for the note I found on the mat when I got home on Saturday.

'Dear Mrs Armitage, I called by to see you, but you were out — hence this note. I've got dreadful news about Mrs Richardson. It seems her mother's died suddenly and she's got to go up to Leeds to sort things out. As you can understand, that puts us in a bit of a sticky position regarding the bazaar — no jams or wines. I was wondering therefore if I could call upon you for assistance, in the way of a few jars of jam and half a dozen or so bottles of wine. You were the obvious choice. After all, the jam does seem to be in keeping with the cakes you'll be making — if you see what I mean, and I happen to know that you make the odd gallon or two of wine. I hope you understand the position I'm in. Much gratitude, Eva Tyson. (The Organiser, St. Jude's Church Bazaar).'

It was true that I'd got some wine in the house, but it needed bottling, and like as not, Eva Tyson would expect pretty little labels and caps on it — more expense — not to mention the time and cost involved in making the jam. I'd just finished reading the note, when there was a knock at the door — the vicar.

'Ah,' he says eyeing the note, 'that looks like Mrs Tyson's handwriting. I bet I can guess what that's about. Yes. Mrs Tyson called to see me last night. I suggested you'd be keen to assist.' There was a funny silence. Then he coughed and said, 'Actually, I've come to ask you a favour myself.'

'Look,' I said, 'it's not exactly the best of times to call, I'm just on my way next door to see to Mr Renshaw's tea. You know he's not able to look after himself at the moment?'

'Yes, I had heard something to that effect. No matter — I'll come with you if you like and see Mr Renshaw myself. I'll explain the problem while you get his tea ready. That way we can kill two birds with one stone.'

What it boiled down to was that he didn't see how he could get round to making enough corn dollies in time for the bazaar. 'They're very time-consuming,' he says.

'Yes, I'm sure, but I don't really see how I can help.'

'Well,' he says, following me up the stairs, 'I thought that possibly, if I were to show you the rudiments, you might be able to lend a hand in your free time.'

Free time! I could have hit him with the tray.

'I don't mind,' comes this voice from the bed. 'I used to make a lot of them at one time. It'll give me something to do while I'm out of action.'

The vicar then burbles on about how splendid it all is and how he'll drop the corn off the next day. Mind you, I thought it was pretty splendid too. At least it meant less work for me. God bless you, you old sod, I thought.

Less work? That's a laugh! We've had water everywhere since he's got to soak the corn before he can make anything. Then, after he's finished for the day, I've had to vac the bits of chaff and stalk out of the bed. The only good sign is that at last he's able to get himself into a chair while I do the cleaning up.

I had another note from Eva Tyson yesterday. Funny how she never seems to be able to catch me at home. It appears that Brian and Grace Stoker are having trouble collecting all the second-hand books, clothes and records.

'I feel sure that I can count on your stalwart assistance. All help, no matter how slight, will be appreciated. Much gratitude, Eva Tyson. (The Organiser, St. Jude's Church Bazaar).'

Anyway, I happened to mention it to Jack last night and he says he'll be happy to take me round in his van a couple of nights a week so we can pick stuff up. He's also offered to help me with the jam-making and wine-bottling. That's a blessing I didn't expect.

Things have been going reasonably well. In addition to picking up the second-hand items, we're also able to sell a few tickets for the tombola as we go from house to house. I must say, it is funny to watch Jack at work pushing tickets onto people. It's all, 'Good evening sir. Good evening madam.' And all the time his little beige trilby's bobbing up and down. He's slick all right. I sometimes think they buy a ticket just to get him off the doorstep. Then every time he gets a sale he turns to me, winks, waggles his eyebrows in the most peculiar way and gives me this really soapy grin. Looks just like a drunken sailor.

Mind you, I hope he's not getting the wrong idea about things. Last night I just happened to say how grateful I was for his help and he reaches into his inside pocket, pulls out his wallet, then plonks this card in my hand.

J. S. Fletcher, Esq.,
The Larches, Cotes Avenue,
Emsthorpe

'Just in case you should every need me,' he says. Then he writes his phone number on the back. 'Ex-directory you know. More confidential.'

'I see.'

'Remember — help is just a phone call away, night or day.'

Soft beggar.

Well, the good news is that Mr Renshaw's back on his feet again. He's not exactly dashing about but at least he's able to wash, dress and feed himself. Which means all . . . *all!* I have to do is clean the house for him.

Things are looking good on the bazaar front too. The jams are all jarred, the wine's all bottled, I've baked a dozen fruit cakes, there are books and records piled in every corner, and I've got more second-hand clothes than Oxfam. Not to mention the regiment of corn dollies Mr Renshaw made, nor the fact that I could re-paper Buckingham Palace with the tombola tickets we've sold.

The only blot on all this is Jack. I had a very embarassing time last night putting him straight on how we stand. The randy sod. We'd just finished shifting the last of the books and records into the lounge.

'But you can't have helped noticing the way I look at you,'

17

he whines. All I could think of was that drunken sailor face of his. I couldn't stop myself laughing. Anyway, he strides to the door, turns to me and says, 'You have my card, I believe,' and then he leaves. So it looks as though that's that.

This last week has brought changes. First change is that the tombola drum is no longer in the lounge; it's now in the kitchen. Second change is that I am no longer cleaning for Mr Renshaw; he's now cleaning for me. The tombola drum is in the kitchen because that's as far as I carried it before slipping a disc. And Mr Renshaw is now cleaning for me because . . . well, I needn't go into that.

The vicar came by again last night, said how sorry he was about my accident but that I was lucky because it could have been worse, said that The Organiser sent her best wishes and wanted me to know that naturally she would not expect me to take any further part in the bazaar.

'And,' says the vicar, 'she assures me that you need have no further worries about the tombola — she is more than willing to draw all the numbers herself.'

Well, that was a weight off my mind.

'Still,' he says, 'work goes on for the rest of us. After all there's the second-hand books, records and clothes to be moved from here, and the jams, the cakes, the bottles of wine, the corn dollies . . .'

'The tombola drum . . .' I sighed.

' . . . And the tombola drum. Mr Stoker is very busy, you know, and we'll never be able to get it all inside his van. Then there's Mr Lever — he's still short of a tenor for the barbershop quartet. And from what I can gather, one of Mr Quigley's morris dancers has a sprained ankle. I don't know how Mrs Tyson's going to cope with it all.'

'I think I've got the answer,' I said, reaching for my purse on the bedside cabinet. I handed him Jack's card. 'Give this to Mrs Tyson.'

He looked at the card. 'Is he willing to help?'

'Night or day,' I said wearily. 'Night or day.'

QWERTYUIOP

Michael Yates

'I know you'll like it here, girls,' said Mrs Baslow, 'it's such a nice new building. Very clean.'

It was also nine storeys high and the Elmdale School of Commerce occupied the whole of the top floor. They had had to move from their old premises, a former Methodist Junior School, only last year when the council voted to demolish it and build a sports centre. But there had been one of those frequent disagreements with the government over monies available. The Methodist School had now become a peace centre, providing cheap coffee and the use of a duplicator for the portion of the unemployed who were active in the fight against nuclear weapons.

'One of the nice things here,' said Mrs Baslow 'is that you can see right across to the town hall from this window — where that red bus is.'

The dozen or so girls moved as one to the window, scanning the bleak autumn morning outside. But the bus had turned the corner.

The girls were not really girls. They were women; young and not so young. However, it was Mrs Baslow's way to refer to them as girls because she was to be their teacher and she knew the importance of establishing her authority.

Mrs Baslow could not be mistaken for a girl. She was 47 years old, a grandmother since Easter, and had been at the School of Commerce for 18 years. She was tall and broad-shouldered. Her breasts, which in undress hung like out-size bean bags, assumed the shape of rugby balls within the confines of the cantilevered bra she habitually wore under her navy blue crimplene suit. To complete an already formidable picture, she wore brown tortoise shell spectacles on a string of multicoloured beads and carried a green leather shoulder bag, with compartments from which thrust a varied collection of pencils, erasers, manuals and textbooks. If Mrs Baslow had ever been a girl, she had long ago renounced her girlish ways in the interests of her profession.

She led them into a classroom. 'This,' she said, 'is the classroom.'

They looked politely on the classroom, but with less urgency than when they had pursued the red bus. As with all classrooms, there were chairs, desks and a blackboard on rollers. On top of each desk sat a typewriter.

'There are books in some of the drawers,' said Mrs Baslow. 'Not enough to go round though. I have a few extra ones but some of you will have to share. You may, of course, buy your own books from the school shop. It's up to you.' Her smile suggested it would be a good idea.

Warily, the girls began to arrange themselves; shy ones to the back, pushy ones to the foot of the dais where stood Mrs Baslow's desk. The middling ones who were left pushed down typewriter keys and slid open drawers before deciding where to settle.

One of them suddenly exclaimed — 'There are no electric ones, Mrs Baslow!'

'Ah,' said Mrs Baslow. Her smile extended to the width of reassurance. 'That's because we want you to get used to all kinds of typewriters — not just the latest models. Some of you, when you get jobs, will be joining small firms who simply can't afford expensive electrical equipment. You wouldn't want to take your driving test in a car with automatic gears now, would you?'

'But will we get the chance to use electric?'

'Oh yes. Later on. I'm sure you will.'

What Mrs Baslow told them next was designed to put them even more at ease. She explained that the school prided itself on its good relations with students, that most of their students were private students of course, but everyone was treated the same and students like themselves — slightly older ones, unemployed people on a government retraining scheme, people whose fees were paid by the welfare state, people who were actually being paid a handsome weekly allowance for coming to school — could be assured of the very best attention, the highest standards of teaching. Bearing in mind, of course, that the typing and shorthand curriculum which normally took two years had been encapsulated, in the interests of the taxpayer, into a mere six months. It would be hard work, with regular tests each week to keep them up to scratch and the occasional special test thrown in without warning — so look out!

· But if there were any problems, real problems, she would always be there with a helping hand to answer any questions. She concluded by having them all recite their names — repeating each Christian name herself, and warned them strongly against the habit of wearing jeans, since they were training for an office after all, and not a factory.

When Susan got back to the detached Georgian style house in Flockton that she and Alec called home, she found it strangely difficult to distil the essence of the day's events.

She had always prided herself on being an acute and articulate observer with a talent for mimicry; had even considered an acting career before getting three A levels and opting for a training course as a librarian. Boyfriends always told her she had the looks — fashionably high cheekbones, wide set eyes, broad mouth and straight blonde hair. And even if her nose was a bit long and her legs a bit short for perfection, at least the flaws gave her character. It was a common interest in theatre that had brought her and Alec together in their student days.

Whenever she came home from watercolour classes, pottery classes, embroidery classes, even upholstery classes (though she had found the work too physically demanding after a couple of weeks), she had always been able to provide an informative and amusing account. Describing in vivid detail the technical processes, recounting one or two anecdotes, catching the style and accent of her fellow students. And Alec, for his part, had always been the perfect audience — knowing when to stay silent, asking intelligent questions about why they did so-and-so or how they managed such-a-thing.

Susan, of course, performed a similar service for him when he returned from a day of lecturing on Wordsworth or arranging the sword fight for the third year drama project's Hamlet. He seemed hardly changed since those early days — still the lean boyish face and clear blue eyes that first attracted her. Though his hair, worn long and brushed forward in the early sixties style, was now noticeably thin.

Mutual support, a sharing of experience — that, she often thought, was why their marriage worked so well.

So why she should suddenly feel tongue-tied was inexplicable. This time the material had been so rich. That preposterous Mrs Baslow going on about jeans! And the way those other girls — those other *women* — seemed to take it all in!

'It's going to be a bit of a hoot,' she told Alec, and he laughed in anticipation. But when it came to stringing all the little impressions together, she was left with dangling sentences, vain gropings for just the right word that would convey it all; Alec leaning forward eagerly in the white leather armchair offering a well-timed, 'Yes I see.'

She told him how, when they had had to type, without looking at the keyboard, Mrs Baslow had actually said — 'No peeping now!' She showed him the piece of paper on which she had intended to type *My name is Susan Constable. I am 38 years old* — and it had come out *Mt ba, eid sUnan Ccobtabel,.*

She showed him the sentences they had had to copy from the typing book, giggling as she recited, '*Diana said killing in pain was a sin. Iain fails in singing, Gillian in hiking. Jack fled for his life on dirty dark roads. Idleness is foolish, learn a good skill. Dirty dense fog fell on hills and dales alike. The crazy paving was fixed by the jolly gardener. Diana has a keen head and lean hands.* Could this have any connection,' she mused, 'with her forthright moral condemnation of agonised homicide?'

'Yes, I see,' said Alec on a more serious note, 'but I hope you can stand this sort of thing. I know how tedious it will be for someone of your intelligence.' He took her hand with his usual tenderness.

She laughed. 'Don't forget I'm getting paid for it. It's the first money I'll have earned since . . . well, it's nine years now. At least it will pay for the studio to be redecorated. I need somewhere to do my watercolours. I don't want it looking like . . .'

'. . . A nursery?' he put in.

'A spare room,' she corrected him. 'Anyway, this course is just what I need. And I might get a real job at the end of it.'

Next day at mid-morning break, the girls proceeded with the serious business of categorising each other. Problems of territory had all been sorted out on the first day; each girl was settled at her own desk with her own chair. As for property: the names of the lucky ones were scribbled on the flyleaf of the available text books and reliable typewriters marked with a discreet scratch on the underside. Now it only remained to look around for suitable alliances.

The one called Pat claimed to know about the hot drink machines. She collected their money and went off with a wooden tray that she had discovered in another classroom. She was one of those whom Susan had described in detail to Alec — dwelling on her chunky hand-knit jumpers and surfeit of jewellery. She claimed to be 30, but looked considerably older.

'Have you tasted that machine tea?' someone asked after Pat had gone out.

'That's why I'm having the chocolate. Chocolate's pretty safe.' The speaker was Liz, a plump brunette of around Susan's age, already revealed as a former teacher of French, divorced, and living with a trainee milkman of twenty-three. Half a dozen girls were clustered round her desk. She had given up looking for teaching jobs long ago, she said. The only thing she'd been offered in the past eighteen months was a job with the British Consul in Zaire. 'But if I left England, I'd miss the climate.'

Sally, in her early twenties, also divorced and the mother of a two year old called Harrison, said she wouldn't mind a change of climate. 'It's bloody cold in here.' She added that being a teacher must be very interesting. 'All I ever did was make up wages — so I took the voluntary redundancy.'

'I think we ought to complain,' said Susan, 'about the heating, I mean.'

'You do the complaining then,' said a thin dark woman in her early thirties, the only one still wearing jeans.

The door opened and there was Pat with the drinks. 'Now, what have I missed?' she asked. 'I can see we're all having a lovely chat.'

The woman in jeans, in what Susan would describe later as a broad voice, was explaining how she came to be on the course. 'It's what you'd call force of circumstances. I need the cash for little luxuries like bread and dripping.'

Some of them laughed.

'Don't you have any ambitions?' asked Sally.

'I don't call it ambition to be at the beck and call of some man for eight hours a day, making little squiggles in a book and him breathing over your shoulder.'

The woman in jeans lit a cigarette. Susan was about to point out the No Smoking sticker on the window, when Pat interrupted.

'Well, nobody's forcing me!' she said indignantly. It wasn't that she didn't like being home with Arthur, Anthea and Dominic. But now the two youngsters were older, it did them good to do things for themselves. And anyway, every married woman should have an outside interest — something to keep her fresh. 'It's a way of . . .' she sucked in her breath groping for the words, '. . . of keeping the magic alive — so the husband benefits as well. And I think the husband should have an outside interest too — so it keeps the magic alive for the wife.'

'I'd always know if our Des had an outside interest,' said the woman in jeans. 'He'd start wearing clean underpants.'

Now Susan remembered her name. It was Frankie, probably short for Frances, though it wasn't really shorter at all.

'There's no need to be vulgar,' said Pat.

'But work,' said Susan, seeing an opening, 'work is a man's interest, isn't it? I think it should be the same for woman. We have just the same right to an interesting job as men have. I used to work in a library . . .'

'I don't think stamping books all day is very interesting,' said Sally. She had put her coat on by now. 'My Brett worked in a hospital. He was a porter. That's not very interesting either.'

Susan tried again. 'But it *is* interesting — being in a hospital. You're so close to the reality of life and death and suffering. It makes you realise what life's about.'

Sally looked unconvinced. 'All he ever talked about was picking up dirty dressings and emptying pigswill and how they bring in the road crash cases with their eyes hanging out. It put me off my tea.'

'Well, it would,' said Pat, 'people's eyes hanging out. I don't think that's what life's about. Not people's eyes hanging out.'

'But it's not about the jolly gardener fixing the crazy paving,' said an exasperated Susan. She hoped they would smile, but no-one did.

'That's only the start,' said Pat, 'if you read the whole book, you'll see the sentences get harder and they tell you all sorts of things. There's things about parliament and foreign countries and the Royal Family and how poetry is good for you.'

A fat girl at the back of the room suddenly called out — 'I think it's boring. I think this whole place is boring. I think life is boring anyway. I've tried to kill myself twice.'

'That's Sandra,' said Pat as though in explanation. Unlike Mrs Baslow, she had remembered everyone's name at first hearing. 'It was only a cry for help, wasn't it?' she shouted back. But the fat girl turned away.

Susan gathered her thoughts. 'Shorthand is what I'm really looking forward to. It's like learning another language, isn't it? And typing may be boring but it's very useful. I can start typing Alec's notes for work.'

That was a mistake. Frankie asked what her hubby did and she had to admit he was a lecturer in English and drama at the polytechnic — though she actually used the word teacher instead of lecturer. And Susan wished she hadn't mentioned drama; English by itself was safe, an ordinary school subject.

'Very nice,' said Frankie. 'And no kids to mither you, I'll bet. I can see you don't need the money.'

'I'm doing it because I want to get a job,' Susan explained. 'A job gives a woman independence. It makes her equal.' She was suddenly regretting the drift of the conversation and her own prominent part in it. What bothered her most was that she had started to introduce ideas into their talk — and she knew from experience that some people resented this. She was quite sure that this Frankie was a person who resented ideas.

'I had you pegged as a women's libber,' said Frankie, 'even before I knew what your hubby did.' She blew a smoke ring and broke it with her finger. 'I don't want your equality, love. D'you think I'd want to be equal with our Des? Equal with a lorry driver that brings home ninety quid a week? Give it a rest. I'm superior to our Des. If I ever left him, all he'd eat would be boiled eggs and cheese on toast because that's all he can make for himself. I don't want to be equal with Des — and I don't want our Lee to be when he grows up. I'm bringing him up like a girl, to have more sense.'

'I cut my wrists the second time,' shouted the Sandra girl. 'I've still got the scars.'

'I think,' said Pat, 'this talk has got very personal.'

'I'm going to look at the homework,' said Liz. 'I don't want to be up past midnight tonight. Barry's got his round to do.'

The girls drifted back to their desks and Susan opened a book. She would certainly complain about the heating, she decided. When she had a moment.

That night, the first night of shorthand, of looking up symbols, copying outlines, getting the thickness right — it was eleven o'clock before she had any time for Alec. But there he was, practically telepathic, with a mug of coffee just when she needed it. They sat on the rug by the radiator, listening to Vivaldi.

'I'd better take my lenses out,' she said when he kissed her. And afterwards, 'As long as I've got you, I know nothing bad can happen.'

'Nonsense,' he said with the right touch of modesty, and laughed.

What did happen to Susan was that she fell hopelessly behind the rest of the class.

At first, the decline was barely noticeable. She had soon realised she was slower than some of the others at typing but put this down to being a perfectionist. Also the inanity of the sentences continued to annoy her when the others appeared not to notice. *'On the shores of Lake Kyanga live Kenya's smallest tribe,* she typed. *'Jack Flash lags while Nifty Nan sells kale. Gales lash lakes as hail slashes hedges. A sad lad has a bad back and a hard head.'*

As for shorthand — she found increasing difficulty memorising the outlines. There seemed no logic to it, and the execution of this or that stroke tugged her fingers away from their natural inclination; the opposite of that principle of streamlining which she had always assumed was central to the whole business.

The method of the School of Commerce was straightforward. If you fell behind, you worked harder. If you drew a wrong outline, you corrected it ten times. If a particular passage gave trouble, you typed it again and again until force of habit made you complete it in the time allowed. If your dictation speed proved too slow, you spent your spare time taking a verbatim note from *Any Questions* or *Letter from America* on the radio. As a result, Susan's homework multiplied alarmingly, spilling over to dominate her weekends as well as her evenings.

'Not to worry,' said Alec cheerily whenever she apologised, 'it'll all be over in a few months.'

She was also doing increasingly badly in Mrs Baslow's weekly tests — part shorthand, part use of English — and only her natural superiority in spelling words like managerial and infrastructure kept her just above the pass mark.

Susan knew from experience that progress in studying was never uniform. You worked and worked, and eventually the breakthrough happened for other girls. How their wrists acquired a new suppleness as they bent over their notepads. How their blind fingers swept unerringly across the rows of keys. No breakthrough came for her.

What came instead was a suspicion that she was looked down on, treated with less consideration than the others. A week before the Christmas break, Frankie complained that the space bar on her machine had stuck. When Liz revealed that the lock on hers had never worked, Susan quickly added that her backspace had become a little temperamental.

'Temperamental?' said Frankie with undisguised scorn. 'Give it a smack then.'

'Remember, girls,' said Mrs Baslow, 'when you get your first job, you'll probably have to use a typewriter that's hardly in the peak of condition. Typists just have to be adaptable.'

'Mrs Baslow,' put in Pat, 'why don't they just swop for the ones going spare? Jenny and Val aren't coming back, so they won't need them.'

This was the first Susan had heard of anyone leaving the course. She had noted two empty seats at the back but assumed that the girls — whom she didn't know very well anyway — were off with colds or similar, something in keeping with the time of year and coldness of the classroom.

Mrs Baslow hesitated, then nodded agreement. 'Frances and Elizabeth — sort it out between you.'

'What about me, Mrs Baslow?' Susan's voice skipped an octave in indignation.

'Yes.' said Mrs Baslow. She gave Susan the look of pained reasonableness that she had used when explaining how they weren't allowed to use the central heating until after Christmas because of the energy crisis. 'I'll see if we can find another machine very soon, Susan. In the meantime, we should try to be philosophical. If you can't use your backspace for corrections you may well find you'll make fewer mistakes.' She smiled, clapped her hands and ordered the class to take out their shorthand notebooks.

The next blow came after Christmas. Susan returned to discover from a predictably well-informed Pat, that three more girls had left. These were: Eve, the mother of a ten-year-old mongoloid whose home life was mainly taken up with keeping her offspring continent; Pauline, married to a woodwork teacher whose objections to her desire for any sort of learning took the form of tearing up her homework; and Debbie, whose dyslexic spelling had kept her weekly marks below Susan's. These three, with their special problems, had been the last buffer between Susan and bottom of the class.

She considered giving up too. She broached the subject with Alec, so patient over her recent neglect of him. To her surprise, he agreed.

'If it makes you unhappy, stop doing it.'

It would have been better if he had debated with her, protested that she was halfway through the course already, that the extra money was coming in handy, that she was exaggerating her failure.

'It's just that it's leading me nowhere,' she said. 'Anyway, even if I qualify, I'll only end up typing invoices and menu cards and always hoping it'll lead to something better.'

'Something better?'

'Well, not that much better really. Secretary to someone, someone important, someone who can teach me. Some man, I suppose.'

'Teach you what?' Alec looked bewildered.

'About . . . I don't know. Management. Organisation. Making things work. I've never known how things actually work, how things in life get done. It's always been a mystery to me — like electricity.'

'If it's any consolation, I've no idea how electricity works either.'

Susan avoided an encircling arm. 'Tell me something. If I left you, would you live on boiled eggs and cheese on toast?'

'Of course not. I'd go down to the poly. You can get a three-course meal for a pound in the staff canteen.' He patted her bottom to show he knew they were both joking. 'If you want to quit the course, go ahead. It's your own decision.'

'No,' she said, 'I'll give it another week or two.'

Next day she arrived early, hoping to finish a transcription exercise before classes started. Someone else had the same idea.

'Come on in,' said Frankie. 'There's plenty of room.'

Susan smiled, nodded and sat down, keeping her coat on. She searched for something to say. 'Did you have a good holiday?'

'Smashing. And you?'

'It was . . . nice.'

'I know. Quiet. It always is without kids. Our Lee took three days teaching his dad to play space invaders on his digital watch. They don't want to play cowboys and indians these days. It's not bang you're dead — like it used to be. It's megaton-bloody-holocaust or nothing.'

'I don't like it,' said Susan. 'Space invaders *or* cowboy guns. It's all violence of some sort.' She stopped. She was talking ideas again. She took out her books.

'That's the difference between you and me, love. I'm a realist. I'm not always looking to change things, like some. I suppose I'm pleased with what I've got really. I'm pleased with Lee — he's a smashing kid. He'll grow up okay, violence or no violence. And I suppose I'm pleased with Des — he's a smashing kid too.'

'I never know how seriously to take you when you talk about your husband.' Susan weighed her words carefully.

'Well, Des isn't perfect, but he's decent. That's all you can expect really. You should've seen them, some of the burks I used to knock about with. They'd be dancing with you, stinking of Newcastle Brown, singing the words of the record in your ear, and it was always Delilah. Every man I ever went with wanted to be Tom Jones. The things you put up with . . . I could show you the scars.'

Susan recoiled. 'You mean, they used to hurt you, beat you up?'

Frankie laughed. 'It was usually a fair fight. I used to get so mad, then I'd lash out. Because they were men — rubbish men — the sort that real men wouldn't give tuppence for. But just because they were men, they could still go places I couldn't go. Know what I mean? They could always get more money than me digging holes in the road. Unemployment's got its uses, love. It's done for a lot of those bastards, shown 'em they're not God's gift.' Frankie laughed once again and her mood changed. 'What about you? You had a good job once, didn't you? Why'd you give it up?'

'I got pregnant. It didn't last. But by the time I had the miscarriage . . .'

'Burnt your bridges.'

'It was our own fault. You see — I'd been pregnant before . . .'

Suddenly the need to tell was greater than her fear of giving hostages. Greater than the knowledge that, with the coming of an audience, the open, gentle Frankie would recede and the sarcastic edge return to her speech.

'It was when we first started. Before we were married. We should have been more careful. We were very rational, we discussed it and came to a decision. It was the right thing to do. We thought it was. We could never have afforded it on student grants, God knows. But we didn't know there wouldn't be another chance. That the second time, when everything was neat and ready, and the third time and the fourth . . . that they wouldn't work out. We didn't know . . . Oh God!' Susan's hands flew to her face and she let out a cry like a wounded bird.

Frankie, startled, jumped to her feet.

'Don't move!' shouted Susan. 'Don't come any closer! My lens has come out. If it's not on the desk, it could be on the floor. They're easy to tread on.' She fell to her knees and began to grope around, hardly aware that the other girls were trooping into the room.

Mrs Baslow entered, a sheaf of papers under her arm.

'As you know,' she addressed the class, her voice raised to compensate for the clatter of the general arrival, 'the examination is now very close. Just to keep you on your toes, I'm giving you a typing test. I'll come round with the paper.'

As she started down the line of desks, there was a slight crunching sound, heard only by Susan and Frankie.

'But Mrs Baslow,' said Liz, amid the chorus of groans, 'I was hoping to use this morning to practise my S stroke.'

'I'm sure you'll find this test very useful, Elizabeth.'

'Please, Mrs Baslow,' said Susan. She sat transfixed, staring hard in front of her.

'What is it, Susan? We don't have a lot of time.'

'Susan hesitated. She turned her head. Mrs Baslow was a furry blob, all blues and browns. 'You haven't replaced my typewriter. The one with the faulty backspace.'

'Haven't I? Oh dear. There's just not been another machine available. We've had such an influx of private students recently.'

Susan stood. She said: 'I won't take this test unless I get a new typewriter.'

Mrs Baslow sighed. She said. 'Now don't be silly, Susan. You've managed so far . . .'

'And it's January and there isn't any heating.'

'I believe they're having trouble with the boiler. And it's been a very mild winter. Some of you will be getting jobs with small firms who are desperately trying to cut down on heating bills . . .'

'And I'd like to be called Mrs Constable. That's my name.' Susan glanced round the class as she made her announcement, though the faces were all blurs. 'Mrs Constable!' she shouted, 'That's who I am! I'll be thirty-nine in April.'

There was a silence. Eventually Mrs Baslow walked over to Susan. She spoke comfortingly. 'Look, dear, are you ill? If you're ill, you can be excused the test. If it's your time of the month . . .'

Susan choked. A spasm went through her whole body. 'Not ill!' she shouted and banged her fist on the desk. 'The jolly girl is in a dreadful rage!'

'What?' cried Mrs Baslow. 'What did you say?'

'She fumes while teacher talks! She shouts while teacher stares!' Susan spread her arms to embrace the air. 'She fails at typing, jibes at teaching! Shorthand is foolish, learn to paint like Rembrandt!'

A guffaw came from Frankie. She clapped her hands. 'The class is cold and clammy,' Frankie shouted, 'Dense damp develops on desks!'

'Stop it,' said Mrs Baslow calmly, 'stop it at once!'

'Mrs Baslow is a cow,' sang Susan. 'She has big tits and clammy thighs!'

'Stop it!' shouted Mrs Baslow.

'Words are not as worrying as razors on the wrist,' called Sandra from the back.

'Oh God,' said Pat.

'Furious females smash faulty machines!' Susan shoved her typewriter off the desk. It landed with a crash, several keys flying off into the air.

'Aaaaagghhhh!' yelled a maddened Mrs Baslow. She dropped the remaining papers and threw herself at Susan, arms flailing.

Frankie and Liz ran across to pull her off and for several seconds the attention of the class was riveted on the ensuing brawl.

Then Pat called out — 'The window! Sandra! No!'

Sure enough, the fat girl was poised on the window ledge — legs bent beneath her for the jump. She waited till all eyes were turned on her, then heaved her bulk against the window pane and disappeared with a scream through the exploding glass.

The girls moved as one to the window. Sandra lay motionless. An orange smudge on the tarmac below.

'Aaaagghhh!' said Mrs Baslow for the second time that morning.

'It wasn't a cry for help after all,' said Pat, taking out her hankie.

Sheep In A Meadow

Mary Sara

The three sheep stood in a line on the crest of a bank in a field full of buttercups. The largest at the head of the row turned its head towards him, the next lowered its head to graze and the third was about to amble away from him. The buttercups in full bloom dusted the grass with pollen and in the far distance, blue hills were hazed in summer heat below a gentle summer sky.

He could imagine his shoes yellow with the bright dust, his jacket off and shirt sleeves rolled up. Perhaps he was heading for those distant fells, a rucksack on his back and all day to spend alone in the country with only sheep, skylarks and fresh breezes for company.

Such was the simple, nostalgic power of the little painting that he sighed deeply without realising his longing could be overheard.

He had often passed the small gallery on his routine set of calls in the market town. The rural area was not one the other reps wanted but it suited him. The commission rate was not as high per mile covered as those in the built-up areas but his much practised pleasant manner and memory for names and faces meant he was able to keep up with them. And enjoy being able to have quiet lunch stops in pleasant places as well.

Today, with time to spare before the next call, he had paused outside to look in as he always did, but instead of passing had pushed open the door and gone in. He had never been in a private gallery like this before. Winter Sunday outings with his parents to the cavernous municipal gallery to gaze uncomprehendingly at dark altar-pieces and gloomy landscapes had, he supposed, put him off art for life. He felt rather daring to have the nerve to enter this unknown territory that belonged to other kinds of people.

He had seen the woman in charge sitting quietly at a desk in the corner of his walks past and she didn't look as if she would be intimidating or press him to talk, or worse, to buy.

'Buy a picture? You can't afford things like that on your pay.' He could hear his wife's sharp retort, if he had suggested such an out-of-character extravagance.

At his sigh, the woman looked up from her work. 'I thought it was a happy picture,' she smiled at him.

'Oh, it is,' he said, 'it's just that . . .' he paused, unsure whether he could explain what it meant to him and embarassed at being required to comment at all. Before he could continue, she rescued him.

'I suppose it reminds us how little time there is to stand and stare in a sunny field when there is a living to be earned,' she replied. She bent her head to her papers again without offering further conversation.

He moved on to the other paintings, before leaving with a bright and cheery 'Thanks, 'bye.'

He often thought of that sunny field in the weeks that followed. The summer was turning out to be a long hot one, which made the hours on the road sweaty and tiring. As the weeks went by, his wife and family bemoaned the fact that his firm dictated he take his main holiday in the spring or autumn.

Their fortnight in Cornwall in early May had been memorable chiefly for the cold and rain which had kept them either on the move from theme parks to steamy cafes or cooped up in the caravan with quarrelling children. Now they were envious — of neighbouring families setting off with excitement and returning, bronzed and laughing — of the postcards they sent — 'Wonderful weather, in the sea everyday.' He wished they wouldn't send them — or show their photographs when they got back. It only made his wife more dissatisfied; a condition which she no longer bothered to conceal, even from the neighbours.

When they chose their holiday, he had suggested Scotland. Purple mountains, blue lochs and romantic castles seen on calendars had called to him, but the family had all been scornful. No-one they knew went to Scotland.

In his teens he had once enjoyed Youth Hostelling in the Lake District with the school. Though the nearest he had got to recapturing that feeling of limitless skies and freedom in recent years had been from his car, moving swiftly through the landscape between towns and cities, but never part of it.

His wife would not hear of camping or taking the caravan to the countryside — 'What would we do if it rained?' she had said, as if, wherever they went, it was much fun when it did.

Maybe when the boy was a bit older they could go off together, do some fishing or something. It would do him good to be dragged away from the endless computer games and videos he and his friends consumed, even on holiday.

A month later, a dusty breeze fluttered across his sweating face through the open window as he drove again into the familiar town where his afternoon calls were to be made. Lunch first, he decided, then business. Half an hour, a half of shandy and a chicken sandwich later, he found himself on the side street where the gallery was. He paused, looked in through the plate glass window and saw that the exhibition had changed. Instead of landscapes, there was now a roomful of pictures of the sea and boats.

'No harm in having a look,' he thought, 'it was all right last time. No sighing this time though,' he joked to himself.

The pictures were cool and calming after the heat of the day outside. Many had red stickers with 'Sold' written on, stuck to the corners of their glass or frames. He wondered if their buyers bought them instead of bothering to go on holiday. The idea appealed to him.

The woman emerged from a rear room which seemed to be part of the gallery, but which he hadn't noticed on his first visit. She nodded a quiet 'Good afternoon' to him as she seated herself at the desk again. 'There are more pictures in the other room if you would like to browse,' she added.

He acknowledged the information with a nod and, after giving each view of sea and harbour its due, he wandered through to the back room. It was a hotch potch collection of all kinds of subjects — flowers, portraits, street scenes, some landscapes again. Hanging by the window were the sheep in their green and gold meadow, the blue hills still beckoning, the grass still being grazed. He glanced quickly round. Had she meant him to come in and see it again, was she hoping he would buy it, would he have to say something to her, explain why he couldn't? A nervous prickle of sweat started under his arms.

For all his confidence and bonhomie as a successful salesman, he felt uncomfortable in unfamiliar social situations. He knew when to close a sale, how to chat up a buyer with just the right amount of implied flattery, how to smooth away problems over lost orders or mis-directed invoices — but talking to an arty, educated woman about pictures was totally outside his experience. After a minute though, when he found himself still alone, he relaxed and began to enjoy the painting again. He took pleasure in its modest celebration of happy, sun-filled, irresponsible hours as much as he had done the first time, but without the longing for the impossible he had felt then.

'No use crying for what you can't have,' he thought, unconsciously repeating his mother's inevitable reply at birthday and Christmas times when he had asked for a new bike or a pair of special George Best soccer boots rather than ordinary ones.

It wasn't that he wanted to have the picture, more that he wanted just a day like that. One day, alone among fields, out of earshot of traffic and with complete freedom to choose where he should go, what he should do.

'Can I help you, or are you happy just looking?' She had come through without him hearing.

He turned quickly and started to say 'I'm sorry . . .' but she interrupted him with a wave of her hand and an apologetic smile.

'No, I'm sorry I made you jump — please carry on looking for as long as you like. I didn't mean you to feel you weren't welcome to just browse — after all, there's no sign to say you can only have five minutes and then you have to buy one,' she laughed.

Her friendliness and manner put him at his ease. He recognised immediately that it was genuine. He should know, his job required him to be expert at sounding sincere.

Yet he was surprised to find himself saying, 'I'm glad to see this one still here. I'm surprised no-one has snapped it up. You were right, it *is* a happy picture.'

Her face lit up with pleasure. 'You remembered it. How very nice. I'm fond of it and actually quite pleased it hasn't sold — yet,' she added. There was a comfortable silence as they looked at it together.

Eventually, more for something to say than because he really wanted to know, he asked, 'Do you know where it is of?'

As soon as he had said it, he thought how stupid he sounded, as if a field could be somewhere like a view of a bridge or a habour.

Not looking at him, but keeping her gaze on the painting, she said, 'Yes I do, actually. It's up in the Yorkshire Dales not far from Linton, and that's the view towards Hetton Moor in the distance. But I suppose it could be anywhere up there really,' she added hurriedly as she turned away to attend to another visitor.

As summer turned to autumn and half term loomed, the family began discussing where they should go for their third week of holiday. He knew his wife wanted to go somewhere abroad.

'Majorca is cheap at this time of the year,' she said pointedly. To which he sullenly replied that presumably there was a good reason for it — like rain and unheated swimming pools.

He tried not to feel that since he earned the money he should decide, partly because he was basically a decent sort of man and partly because he didn't want the responsibility of getting it wrong. Eventually he surprised them all, and himself, by suggesting they stay at home but each day take trips out: to funfairs, shopping sprees, anything they wanted — so long as he could have one day on his own.

The prospect of the money saved being spent so freely on their various desires won them all over with little argument. And his wife, when he explained he only wanted to go walking on his solitary day, soon lost her suspicions of his motives and began planning where they should go each day.

The week was a great success. New clothes, generous spending money and their reasonable expectations of each outing more than adequately realised lent the family expeditions a relaxed good humour. They went to stately homes, the zoo, ate out at cafes, even a proper restaurant dinner for them all one evening.

For his day he chose the Saturday. He had worked out his route with care, having looked it up on the map weeks before. He would head for Linton in the Dales. His expectations were tempered by an innate commonsense that told him he would not find the buttercup field or probably anything like it. But at least he could walk on grass, sit in the October sunshine and breathe fresh air in solitude.

The day started well with sunshine and a boyish sense of playing truant. It ended with disaster. On the bypass to the town he so often visited for work, his car broke down. It had to be towed to a garage and he was told he would have to wait several hours before they could fix it.

He felt like weeping with disappointment and frustration. His throat ached with anger at the unfairness of life. There was little to see in the town that he had not already seen, and not quite enough time to get a train or bus on to Linton and back again. He had only wanted one day off from earning a living and being a family man — to stand and stare in the countryside. Was it so much to ask? His anger stirred him to a decision. Damn it, he would salvage something from the wreckage of his day.

Entering the gallery, he did so with purposeful strides that took him straight through to the room at the back where, startled, the woman said, 'Oh, hello, can I help?'

'The sheep in the buttercups, have you still got it?' he demanded.

She glanced at the stack of paintings against the wall she had been sorting through. 'No. Well . . . yes . . . I mean . . .'

She was not only startled by his abrupt entrance, but now he saw his question too had caught her off guard.

'Look, either it is or it isn't,' he persisted more calmly.

She looked at him as if she could read something in his face that would help her decide. Then, looking down at the paintings leaning at her feet, she said, 'Yes it is. Here you are,' and she separated it from the rest. 'Yes,' she said again as he held it in his hands. 'It's yours. You seem to need it more than I do.'

Puzzled, he looked from her to the picture and back to her again.

She answered his silent question by telling him that she was the artist. The painting was a record of a moment in a wonderful day she had spent, alone and carefree at a time when such moments were rare in her life. Since no-one seemed to want to buy it, she had more or less decided to take it out of stock and keep it.

'Then you still want it really,' he said, trying to sound generous while desperate with his own need of it.

41

'No. I am very pleased you like it so much. Besides, I will always have the memory of that day in my head. It will be good to know someone else is going to share it. That's the main reason most artists paint, really.'

When he remembered her words later, he thought that from anyone else they would have sounded insincere and he would have insisted she keep it. As it was, he simply smiled his gratitude while he paid for it and she wrapped it for him. He did not trust himself to begin to explain how grateful he was. His throat was aching again, this time with pure delight.

As he headed for home, the painting lying on the seat beside him, he felt that some burden of need which he did not truly understand had been lifted from him. He also knew that it was going to be hard to explain. It was only some sheep in a meadow — as his wife would say. But he could handle that now.

The Journey

by Jean Pearson

I knew as soon as I handed over the taxi fare that I was cutting it fine. It seemed that everything was out to delay me. Red lights, jams, road works, the lot. Anyway, I was here now, but I was going to have to run.

The taxi driver dropped me off by the main entrance to the station. Even at this hour, people were milling in and out onto the main concourse. Of course, it was rush hour — I should have remembered the alterations too. For a minute I was stumped as I looked round frantically for the ticket hall. Damn it, it was now even further from the platforms.

I let myself look at the huge clock over the barriers as I raced through to buy my ticket. Oh hell, less than five minutes and every window had a queue. Did it matter which I chose? Sods' law would make sure that if I chose the shortest, somebody in front would cock it up and cause a delay.

I was in luck. I picked a clerk who seemed to be in as big a hurry as me. With my ticket now in my hand, I ran back through the concourse. Let it be late, please let it be late.

If the clerk had been in a hurry, the ticket collector certainly wasn't. He examined every ticket presented in minute detail. For heaven's sake hurry up. Then it was my turn.

'Which platform for Penzance, please?'

He kept hold of my ticket while he scrutinised the list on his clipboard. Come on, come on.

'It's in now. You're going to have to run — platform seven.'

I grabbed my ticket off him and ran. Platform seven, of

course, was at the other side. Under the subway and up the steps. There it was, engines vibrating the air. The porter slamming the doors shut as he walked its length.

Made it. I was on, thank God. A good job there were plenty of seats, I hadn't had the time to book in advance. I heaved my holdall up onto the luggage rack then gratefully flopped into a seat, tucking my shoulder bag tight into my side.

The carriage was almost empty — just the odd couple spread about. Unsociable lot we are, I thought. And that's how I liked it. The engines roared louder and slowly the train began to glide past the platform. Another minute and I would have missed it. I could now let myself relax. Not too much, mind you, but enough.

The buffet car attendant must have been waiting for the off. Within minutes he was swaying up the aisle. 'Coffee, tea?'

My first cup of the morning. Even in a paper cup, even British Rail, that coffee tasted good.

I still hadn't got my thoughts together. I hadn't expected to sleep last night, not after all the panic. But I had — like a log. That was why everything had been such a rush this morning. I'd nearly slept in and spoiled everything.

What time is it? Ten to eight. He won't be back till at least two. My stomach turned at the thought of Malcolm coming in through the back door and finding me — and it — gone. If it hadn't been for the phone call, I would still have been there, then I would have been the one left holding the baby.

I looked out of the window. We were racing through Wakefield station. Not stopping. I didn't want it to stop. Ever.

It all made sense. You know how it is when you're sure something's going on but you can't explain why you know. It was obvious now — it all added up. There had been too many late nights. A couple of times a week had become normal, but just lately it had been every night. On Friday it had been all night. And no explanations.

'Mind your own business — where do you think I've been? Do I have to ask your permission if I want to stay out? Sorry, lads, you'll have to play without me. I didn't ask the missus.'

Who did he think he was kidding? He hadn't seen the lads for months. I'd bumped into Johnny outside the library only last week.

'How's Malc?' he asked. 'None of the lads have seen him in months.'

I'd wondered if he was up to his old tricks again. He'd promised me faithfully he'd finished with all that years ago and I'd promised what I'd do if he hadn't . . . but it hadn't been this.

Friday had been the day — or night, as it turned out. He came home Saturday morning. In through the back door, swinging his haversack as if nothing was amiss, but I could see he was spoiling for a fight.

'Where have you been all night?' I asked.

'Mind your own business, eh.'

I clattered about the kitchen just making my own breakfast, while he disappeared upstairs. I could hear him in the spare room. What was he doing in there? He came down after a while.

'Any tea going?' he asked, as if everything was all right.

'Help yourself — you're not helpless.'

'Be like that then.'

He poured his tea and buttered himself the crust off the loaf and ambled through into the room. Telly on. That's it for the day.

The train was slowing down. We were approaching Derby. There was a bit of activity in the carriage as the couple at the bottom stood up. He was reaching a bag down, she was struggling into her coat. A thin line of passengers edged the platform, children's hands were grabbed.

Now where was I? Oh yes. I got cleared up early and then I was off out. As I'd slammed the door after me, he'd called 'Where are you going?' Cheeky bugger.

You can't imagine how hard it can be making a trip into town last all day. Normally, it's all rush and I'd give anything for a leisurely day to look around the shops. But last Saturday — I must have wandered round every counter in every shop. And I lost count of the coffees I had. I wanted to go home, but I was showing him.

When I finally got off the six o'clock bus, I was walking up the street and saw him going off in the opposite direction. Out again. Surprisingly, he left everything tidy for once. I could see he'd had some dinner. He'd washed up and put the things away, but just to let me know he'd fended for himself, he left the empty frozen meal packet on top of the fridge.

I didn't bother waiting up for him. I didn't lie awake listening for him either, but it must have been well into the early hours when he came home. He wasn't there when I went to the bathroom at two.

He stayed in all Sunday. Sprawled on the settee with the papers. We ate our dinners in silence, then he was back to the settee, the telly and sleep. Pig. He didn't go out Sunday night either. He got off the sofa only to go to the bathroom and once to make a phone call in the hall. He shut the door after him and was whispering. I stopped trying to listen after a minute. Let him get on with it.

I didn't go into work Monday morning. It wasn't that I didn't feel well, but I didn't feel quite right. Was there any wonder? Malcolm said he might be working over — wouldn't be home until about six. Kind of him to tell me.

Birmingham already — New Street. Plenty of people getting on here. Hope nobody sits near me. Lots of doors banging, people pushing up and down the aisle. The whistle and off again. The carriage is almost full now. Still,

I got my wish. Nobody came to my table. I wonder why, then sink back into my thoughts.

I must have been asleep in the chair doing a Malcolm, when the phone rang. It made me jump. Who'd be ringing this time of day? I'd rung my excuses to work, it wouldn't be them and nobody else knew I was home.

I couldn't be bothered. I tried to ignore it but it was persistent. My book slipped off my knee as I stood up and went into the hall. As I picked the phone up, she started straight away. I didn't even get chance to say hello.

'Hello, Malcolm,' she said. 'I have to be quick while the boss is out. There's still hell on here but I managed to get out to the travel agent and got the tickets like you said. You hardly gave me enough money though — but I managed. After all, we're rich now, aren't we love?' she giggled. 'Come straight round with your things after tea tomorrow. Better make it all look normal — you don't want your Pat to twig on.' She laughed. 'I'm off now, Jim's coming back. See you.' She blew a kiss then hung up.

I hadn't said a word. I couldn't. I was speechless.

What was he up to? *'After all, we're rich now.'* We're rich now — what did the bitch mean?

I had a sudden thought and raced straight upstairs to the spare bedroom. What had he been doing in here? I turned every drawer over in the dressing table, frantic. Nothing, just spare sheets and pillow cases. The wardrobe! Where had he put the key? I flew into our bedroom. The keys to the big wardrobe were still in the locks. Fool. He'd forgotten the keys fit both. My hands were trembling as I turned the key. Whatever it was, it was in here.

The guard's voice quickly brought me back to reality. 'We are now approaching Bristol Temple Meads. The next station in a few minutes will be Bristol Temple Meads.'

Funny, I'd not heard him announce the other stations. Spend a penny quick, I thought, in case the train fills up here. I hurried along to the end of the carriage, my bag tight under my arm. I had to be quick, I felt the train slowing and people were standing in the aisle collecting their belongings together. I shot the bolt across the door and caught a sudden glimpse of my face in the fogged-up mirror. I look as if I'm running a temperature or had too much sun. Too much sun in April!

I just managed to get back to my seat as the brakes screeched the train to a standstill. I guessed right. The train was filling up. Lots of naval uniforms — bound for Plymouth, I bet. I put my coat and a newspaper I picked up onto the seat beside me. Make it look as though this seat is occupied, I decide, as a young couple seem intent on taking the seats opposite me

'Are these seats taken?' asks the girl.

I just shake my head in answer. Then they make a palaver about rolling coats up and putting them on the luggage rack with their bags. Before the train even sets off, out come the flask and sandwiches.

I suddenly realise I'm hungry. Lunchtime and I'd only had a coffee and a biscuit. No wonder. Saved again. The attendant must be telepathic. There are two of them, one pushing the trolley while the other goes in front touting for custom. I'll have another coffee and a plastic wrapped cheese sandwich, and just in case I'm still hungry, a piece of dirty-yellow coloured slab cake.

It's lovely. And the young girl, eyes closed, now has her head on his shoulder. Isn't love wonderful?

He'd stuffed it all into my winter boots standing at the back of the wardrobe, hidden behind the big coats. As soon as I picked one up, I knew.

I sat on the floor shaking the contents out of the boots onto the carpet, heart thumping and hands shaking. My God, she was right. We're rich now. The money was in bundles — ten, twenty, fifty pound notes. I tried to count it and gave up. I kept losing count, but there was a lot. A hell of a lot.

Funny. The idea came instantly. I didn't even have to think. I raced downstairs and grabbed Sunday's paper and magazines and sat on the bedroom floor tearing them to pieces and shoving them into the boots — my beautiful big boots.

I fetched the holdall up from under the stairs and threw a few undies and toiletries in, then put it back where I got it from. Then there was a frantic search for my big shoulder bag. I needed a big bag.

I had Malcolm's tea all ready for him when he came in from work. I'd fetched a bit of steak and managed to get a few very expensive Jersey potatoes. When he came in through the back door, he looked surprised.

'What's this, my birthday?'

I smiled at him. 'I thought you deserved a treat, love. You don't get many.'

I put his dinner on the table and he sat straight down to it. Didn't even bother to wash his hands. I picked up his haversack and newspaper from the floor and put them on the washer top. My eyes caught the headlines as I did so — *Local Supermarket Robbery.*

I sat opposite while he ate. Trying not to look anxious, I watched his every move. But I needn't have worried. After his dinner, he was content to sprawl on the settee, his coffee on the floor beside him. He felt safe.

My heart had stopped every time he went upstairs, but thankfully he didn't go into the spare bedroom. He'd leave his preparations till it was too late.

He snuggled up, all affectionate like, when we went to bed. He kissed the back of my neck. I guess he was feeling sorry for me.

When I got up at six, he'd already left for work. For an awful minute, I thought I'd slept in. I got dressed in a hurry and rang for a taxi. I could hardly keep myself still for shaking. I nearly died when the taxi pipped its horn. Don't wake the street up.

I didn't leave a note. Not a proper one. I just drew a question mark in thick felt pen across that article in the paper and left it in the wardrobe.

The train is running alongside the sea towards Dawlish and Teignmouth — my favourite bit. The afternoon sun is out and sparkling like diamonds on the sea. I lay back in my seat and smile. The young couple are leaning forward, excitedly pointing to boats and surfboarders — like little children.

We won't be long now. Then a new beginning.

Up A Nick In Briggate

Brenda Scott

'Cheers, Bill. Merry Christmas, love.' Ma raised her glass towards her son-in-law who was deep in contemplation of the froth atop his pint.

Bill's wife Peg glanced up from her port and lemon, eyebrows arched. 'Not much chance of that is there, Ma?' she said curtly.

Peg was at best a bit of a pessimist. No spark, no love of life for its own sake, face like a wet weekend. Bill's eyes drifted from the murky depths of his pint pot as he thought, not for the first time, about the vagaries of life that had led him to nestle in the bosom of his strangely incongruous family : old Ma Woodford the matriarch, stout and stiff and willing to unbend only after the third rum and pep had slithered down her throat; Dad, quiet and unassuming, living in the past and searching, ever searching, for the far-off days of glory when, as a private in the Camel Corps, he had ridden the sands of the desert and seen the world through bluer eyes. Too old now to be much use.

This was a different kind of war. A man disappointed, withdrawn, saddened that he had never managed to get himself sons to see the glory for him, to do their bit, to give him back his pride. No sons, just two daughters filling magazines for Bren guns and complaining about bloody rationing and the lack of stockings. Two daughters and two sons-in-law, both in reserved occupations at the forge and the mill. No glory there. Bill took a long pull at his pint, feeling something of the old man's disappointment and shame.

'Fancy another, Dad? Joe?'

Bill stood up, sweeping their empty glasses into his big hands, not waiting for their answer as he made his way to the bar. Better get one in for the women as well. The pub was half empty, most of the regulars were away and those that were on leave, if they had any sense, would be enjoying the delights of the ale across the way in the Rising Sun. He returned to the table with the full glasses and belched discreetly.

Peg frowned at him. 'Bill, really!'

'Pardon me.'

He returned to the depressing study of his glass. Peg's grandmother on her mother's side, had managed to get herself killed by a Sammy Ledgard's bus while crossing the road to buy her nightly gill from the Sun. The bus driver hadn't realised that she was wrapped round his front wheels until he was halfway down the road to Kirkstall Abbey. By which time, it was too late. Ninety-two years old, she'd been. Bill reckoned she'd had a bloody good innings and that her family should let bygones be bygones. Let the old trout rest in peace. What was left of her. But no, they had boycotted the Sun ever since.

Rumours had circulated, radiating from the snug via the taproom and thence to the rest of Kirkstall Road, that old Sal had met her end on the way back from the off-sales, having downed more than a few in the meantime. Which explained why the daft old bugger hadn't seen the double decker until it was nearly on top of her. Well whatever, at least she'd had the good sense to patronise the off-sales at the Sun and not here, in this dingy hole where the beer was so full of gas it would float a dirigible.

Bill belched again, louder this time, just for the hell of it. Peg tutted, her lips pursed. Sitting beside her, Phyllis, her sister, giggled and leant forward.

'Bill, really!'

It was by way of a sidesweep at Peg. Like chalk and cheese those two. Phyllis wasn't the type to let anything get her down, not even this bloody war. Not even if it meant having Joe under her feet every night when he came off firewatch duty, intent on telling her in his lugubrious style of every little insignificant event. Clucking round her like a bloody mother hen imparting titbits of gossip, for all the world like a woman with nothing better to do. At least Bill had a bit of go about him. She liked a man with a bit of go. Peg didn't appreciate much at all. Phyllis's cherry lipstick echoed the shape of her mouth on the glass as she drank. Merry bloody Christmas.

Bill glanced across at his father-in-law and grinned. 'What about this head then, Dad? Do you think they'll find it?'

The old man's eyes lit up. This was his favourite topic of conversation. It stopped him dwelling on the war. 'Dunno, Bill. They've not had much luck so far. It'll be in t'Aire, mark my words. Probably rotted by now, I shouldn't wonder.'

'Nay, they'd have found it by now.' Joe put in his two-pennorth for what it was worth. 'I've watched 'em, see, every day for a fortnight, mucking about down by the bank. They've found nowt.'

Joe spoke with his habitual air of quiet authority, as one who knows. Didn't he work at the mill, its windows overlooking every aspect of the river as he overlooked its workers? He should know. They'd found nowt.

'Well it must be somewhere.' Phyllis puffed elegantly on her cigarette, leaning forward, elbows on the table. 'It makes me come over all queer just thinking about it!' She shivered coyly.

'Don't think about it then,' her sister said, wondering why her family had this obsession with gore. Wasn't there enough blood and muck in the world without raking around in the dirt for more? And on Christmas Eve as well!

'The feller who did it must be some kind of pervert,' Bill continued, getting into his stride. 'I mean, fancy cutting her up into all them pieces. Must've taken him ages.'

'I've got a nice piece of hock for tomorrow,' said Ma absently.

Peg latched onto her comment by way of a diversion from the men's distasteful conversation. She didn't want to know what that evil bugger had done to the girl after he'd done her in. It was what he'd done beforehand that turned her stomach. Filthy swine.

'I've made a nice cake, Ma. Me and Phyllis clubbed together our coupons for the extra. I've used some gravy browning to give it a bit of colour.' She paused to look round the room. 'I'll be glad when this bloody war is over.'

'And then they say he must have strangled her with her own stocking and pulled it so tight her face turned blue and puffed up like a balloon.' Dad was well into his stride and his fifth pint by now.

'Lucky she could get stockings.' Phyllis's tone was one of envious disgust. She turned to Peg. 'I hope you didn't use all that gravy browning.'

Joe had promised to take her to the Empire on Boxing Day. She didn't want to be seen in the foyer during the interval with winter white legs. Not in the Empire. Such a nice class of customer they got in there. Refined like.

Outside, the rain, mizzling down from a bleak sky, made greasy patches on the pavements. No streetlamps, no headlights, not a chink of light from a badly drawn blackout curtain. Nothing to show for Christmas, save in the distance, the faint discordant warbling of a small bedraggled group of youngsters, They were carolling their tuneless way stoutheartedly from door to door in the vain hope of a penny or a warm mince pie.

Down by the river, the fog rose, clammy and close. Up a nick in Briggate two men met, spoke hurriedly into the stillness of the night, and, shaking hands, parted again. The fog closed in.

'Come on, Joe, sup up. It's chucking out time.'

Obligingly, Joe raised his glass to his lips, draining it. He placed it neatly on the cardboard mat and rose.

'I'll just nip for a quick jimmy riddle,' said Bill and disappeared in the direction of the Gents.

Phyllis stifled another giggle. The look on Peg's face was a picture.

Peg shuffled into her coat, noticing that Phyllis only had to glance at her Joe as she held out her arms stiffly behind her and he did the honours. Bill always managed to disappear at times like these rather than be gallant. He never opened doors for her either. Oh well, she philosophised inwardly, at least he was here. Mustn't grumble. If he'd been killed in action, she'd have nothing left to grumble about.

It was still drizzling as they stepped out into the night, blinking to acclimatise their eyes to the darkness. All was silent save for Phyllis's high heels clicking rhythmically on the flags. The carol singers had long gone home to their beds. Huddled together, they made their way towards Roseberry Terrace, aided only by the dull glow of the men's tab ends.

From the doorway of the pub they heard sounds of farewell resonate in the stillness.

'Night, love!'

'Night, love! Merry Christmas!'

'Night, love!'

Bill reckoned he could hear them still singing in the Sun and let out a sigh.

The fog enclosed them as they turned the corner by Milford Place. Footseps echoed behind them, coming closer, moving fast. Someone running. They could hear his breath as his lungs gasped for air.

'Ay up then, what's this?' Bill's voice sounded loud, strident.

The women closed ranks, instinctively protective. The man didn't stop, just hurled himself into their midst, scattering them as a fox would a huddle of chickens.

'Here, watch it, mate!' Joe made an attempt at bravado.

Phyllis gave a little scream, high pitched yet ladylike.

'Take this mate and see what you can do with it. The buggers are after me.'

Still moving, caught in the vortex of their bodies, the man pushed Joe aside, breaking through their circle. They could hear his shoes slapping on the pavement as he ran hell for leather towards the river. Faintly, in the distance, a policeman's whistle sounded its alarm. A distinctive, urgent note.

For a while they stood there, stunned into silence. Then, slowly regaining their bearings, they set off towards Ma's place. The door wasn't locked. No point, when you've got nowt worth pinching. They trooped in, and only when the door was shut behind them did Dad switch on the light. In the brightness of the room they moved as one towards the table.

Peg glanced at Bill. 'Well, what is it? What did he give you?'

Bill put the parcel in the centre of the table and they moved closer to get a good look. It was wrapped in brown paper and tied roughly with string. A brownish red fluid seeped ominously through the wrapping.

Blood.

Phyllis screamed. 'Oh! Jesus Christ! It's the head!'

The gory package sat there oozing, willing them to take a peek. Peg went white under her face powder.

'It's going all over me best bit of cloth,' Ma observed, her eyes glued to the puddlesome thing.

Bill took charge. 'Come on, this is men's work. You . . .' his glance swept over the three women, '. . . get into the scullery and stay there until we tell you to come out. And put the kettle on,' he said as an afterthought.

Ma and her two daughters cowered by the set pot, eyes full of horror, pupils dilated with excitement.

'I think I'm going to be sick,' Peg whispered. The words

caught up in her throat where an indigestible lump was rising, falling, rising again.

Ma filled the kettle and put a match to the gas. It backfired and they jumped, their nerves jangling.

In the parlour the men gathered closer round the table, their heads bent towards the parcel, excluding the light from the shaded bulb overhead. Bill prodded at it with a stiff finger.

'Well?' Joe asked.

Bill shrugged. His stomach felt tight and his hands were sweating.

'Dunno. It feels sort of softish, squashy like.'

'Stands to reason,' said Dad. 'It'll have rotted away by now.'

Bill reached into his pocket and took out his fags. Silently he passed them round and they lit up, inhaling deeply. A droplet of rainwater ran down the brown paper and lodged on a knot in the string. Blood continued to ooze.

Throwing his tab end on the back of the fire, Bill turned once more to the table. An air of determination hung over him. He straightened his back, feeling his spine clock into place as he pushed back his shoulders. Slowly he approached the parcel.

In the scullery the kettle began to wail.

*

Fred Ackroyd shut the door quietly behind him and bent to remove his boots. Winded, he lowered himself into the fireside chair. He leaned back and closed his eyes, perspiration mingling with the rainwater running in rivulets down his neck. He breathed heavily. Ah well, the buggers wouldn't catch him now, he was safe. It had been a close shave, though. But what a bloody waste of effort. What a bloody waste. He sighed, blowing the air from his aching lungs. Still, that was life, easy come . . . His loss would be somebody else's gain. His natural good humour restored, he permitted himself to smile a little.

*

'By gum, Ma, that was grand!' Bill crossed his knife and fork on his plate and, pushing back his chair, unfastened the top two buttons of his trousers.

Peg picked up his plate and stacked it neatly on top of the others. The meat on her own was hardly touched.

'Best bit of beef I've tasted since afore t'war,' Dad mused. His eyes were moist with emotion as he stared lovingly at the plentiful remains on the big blue and white dish, which sat pride of place, in the centre of the table.

'Aye — and you can take your eyes off it. That'll last us another week if we're careful.' Ma said, picking up the pile of dirty crocks. 'Peg, put it on the cellar head, it'll keep nice in there.'

Peg leaned over and grabbed the dish. 'I'll wash up, don't trouble yourselves.'

She went into the scullery and opened the cellar door. There was the uncooked hock, flaccid and pale, forlorn on its dish. She put the beef beside it.

The men had howled with laughter last night when the parcel had finally been unwrapped, exposing its innards. Black market beef. Red with blood, fresh from the kill and large enough to fill an army. Laugh. They clung to each other and hooted. What a lark. Something to tell the kids when they grew up.

Sprinkling a few soap flakes into the sink, Peg plunged her hands into the suds and stared out of the scullery window. There was a crack in one of the panes and the sash cords were fraying.

Somewhere out there was a head. A head belonging to a girl who hadn't lived to see another Merry Christmas. She wondered vaguely where it was.

In the parlour, the rest of the family were still laughing.

Crabby Uncle Ted

Walt Palmer

Enoch's Uncle Ted was a giant of a man. He spoke with a southern accent and seemed to avoid any work that involved getting his hands dirty. Enoch's dad called him a middle-class burk, and in truth, some of the ventures he launched in an effort to maintain his station in life were hare-brained to say the least. When he talked, especially when in drink, everything was a money-spinner, a gold mine, too good to miss, a once in a lifetime opportunity. And so he acquired a fishmonger's shop together with a motorbike and side car, to set him on the road to fortune.

'What the bloody hell does he want a motorbike for?' Enoch's dad oathed, 'He's not doing deliveries is he?'

His mother rolled her eyes and altered her face into a 'here we go again' expression as she continued ironing and listening to dance music which bubbled from the radio.

'They say every family's got one,' he went on as he poked the fire.

'We haven't got one, Dad,' Enoch said.

'Got one what?' questioned his father.

'A motorbike.'

'I didn't mean a motorbike. I meant a burk,' came the sneering answer.

Enoch turned away and smiled quietly to himself.

'Have you seen the sign he's put up?' Enoch's father continued in a disgusted voice. 'High Class Fish Shop. I ask you, High Class Fish Shop. All his crabs must talk with a posh accent.'

The following evening, Enoch's father returned from work as usual, threw his cap at the nail on the back of the door, missed it as usual, sat down to his tea, and said, 'He's wearing a striped apron now. He looks a right chuff.'

His long suffering wife poured gravy over his potatoes and listened as he muttered his meal away.

Each night when he came home, they were treated to more tit-bits of information regarding Uncle Ted and his fish shop.

'I swear that halibut has been in his window all week. He stands need to call it a fresh fish shop. Half of them around here will go down with food poisoning — you mark my words.'

'Shush, Randolph,' Enoch's mother warned. 'Remember, Enoch's here.'

He bent his head and mumbled into his mashed potatoes while Enoch visualised the black death creeping over all and Uncle Ted being carted away to prison in his blue and white striped apron.

The following evening, his dad burst into the house and stood wide eyed. 'I don't believe it. I don't bloody believe it.'

Enoch's mother glanced up from her task of polishing the lino.

'What's up now?' she sighed.

'What's up? What's up? That half baked brother-in-law of mine. That's what's up.'

'What has he done now?' she asked wearily.

'What's he done? What's he done? I'll tell you what he's done. He's made the family a laughing stock. That's what he's done. There's crabs everywhere. Every-bloody-where. All the cats around here are having a birthday outside his shop. God, he's —'

'Crabs?' Enoch's mother queried.

'Yes, crabs. Hundreds of them. Live 'uns, all over the place. They've escaped from his motorbike. They're running riot. He's mad, Peggy — I'm telling you.'

Enoch slipped from the house and ran excitedly down the road towards Uncle Ted's High Class Fish Shop. He rounded the corner and stopped dead in his tracks. The scene before him was bizarre. Uncle Ted and Auntie Ida were retrieving crabs of all shapes and sizes. Some hid under privet hedges, others scuttled off towards the steelworks. Unfortunate ones had been cornered by neighbourhood cats who found the smell appetising but cound not solve the problem of nipping claws and hard, unyielding shells.

Every so often, there was a high pitched delicate scream as Auntie Ida's fingers were caught in the pincers of a protesting crab.

'Catch the bloody things, woman — don't play with them,' Uncle Ted shouted. 'Pick them up by the arse, not the front.'

Auntie Ida whimpered.

A large glass tank lay on its side in the side car of the motorbike. It was from this that the spidery crabs had sought freedom.

When Uncle Ted had said he was going to sell fresh fish, he had determined to uphold the word *fresh* — to the letter. His journey from Flamborough Head, together with his slopping live cargo, had been hazardous, and to see the fruits of his efforts disappearing at a rapid rate of knots in all directions would have reduced a lesser mortal to despair.

Not so Uncle Ted.

'Fetch a shovel, woman,' he commanded.

Enoch's auntie meekly disappeared into the shop and returned some moments later carrying a small coal shovel.

Together they scooped the crabs into a hessian sack which became animated as it was filled. Soon every crab in the immediate vicinity was captured and they paused to rest.

'If I ever catch the little swines that tipped them out, I'll murder them,' Uncle Ted cursed.

Enoch drew back around the corner. Not because he was guilty, but knowing that an innate thirst for vengeance branded all children equally guilty in the eyes of adults.

Suddenly he heard Auntie Ida's high pitched voice. 'What about the crabs that have disappeared down the road, Ted?'

Uncle Ted replied with a sigh. 'Forget the buggers, they'll find it's a long walk back to the sea.'

The faint tinkle from the shop bell sounded as they returned inside and peace once more shrouded the dusty road.

Uncle Ted's Flamborough crab run became a regular weekly journey. The gang watched him on their way to school as he disappeared down the cobbled road towards the coast. On their way home, he'd pass them on his return journey, the over-heating engine putt-putting and gasping for rest. In the side car, bewildered crabs, who had only that morning been fathoms deep in their North Sea home, peered through glass and perspex windows at the strange sights which slipped by.

The gang paused at the bottom of the road to make plans as to what to do after tea. Various games were suggested but the one that received most votes was to learn some new swear words while they watched Enoch's uncle boiling the crabs.

They met at their usual den and when they were all assembled proceeded to the back yard of Uncle Ted's High Class Fish Shop. The yard was surrounded by a high brick wall which they cautiously peered over. Long before they could see into the yard, they could hear Uncle Ted's voice growling and cursing. In the centre of the yard was a large cast-iron pot boiling away on an equally large gas ring. Uncle Ted had his back to them and was gingerly dropping crabs into the salted water. Occasionally, a crab bobbed to the top and then the novice fishmonger exploded into voluble curses.

'The blinker, the twisting blinker. I'll never buy blinking crabs off that blinking blinker a-blinking-gain.'

Using a scoop, he reached into the pot and removed the

floating bad crab. In blind rage, he threw it at the white-washed wall. Another bobbed to the surface.

'Blinking hell. Not another blinking one. When I see him next week, I'll blinking kick him in his blinkers.'

'That was a good one,' Alan whispered. I'll remember that one. He whispered the word blinker, savouring the sound.

The gang nodded in silent appreciation then returned their gaze to crab-slinging Uncle Ted.

Yet another crab surfaced. Uncle Ted's neck turned bright purple, his hands clenched until his knuckles were white. He threw his head back and roared in the evening sky.

'Blinkers. Blinkers. Blinkers.'

The obscenities echoed around the rooftops and the words deepened further the inferiority complexes of neighbouring kids born out of wedlock.

'He's on form tonight,' Brian whispered.

The rest of the gang nodded their heads in agreement, appreciating the free vocabulary lesson.

Soon the whitewashed wall was smeared with half-boiled, bad crabs and Uncle Ted's profits had taken a terrible tumble. His wife nervously appeared at the rear door.

'What ever's up, love?' she enquired.

'What's up?' Uncle Ted mimicked her northern accent. 'What's up? That's what's up. Twelve blinking bad crabs. That's what's up, woman.'

'Aww Ted, I'm ever so sorry.' She apologised as though it was her fault that the crabs had been suffering from some terminally ill disease.

'Put the blinking kettle on, woman,' he snarled.

Aunty Ida disappeared into the fish emporium.

The smell of boiling crabs wafted on the warm summer air, drawing cats from miles around. Soon the opposite wall was crowded with moggies, each one salivating and staring down into the amphitheatre of Uncle Ted's open-air kitchen.

'Ted, Ted,' Ida's voice called.

Ted gave the pot a final vigorous stir, sighed anew as he viewed the sacrificial wall, turned, and entered the shop. The gang stared down into the empty yard, their eyes mesmerised by the bubbling crab-filled water.

Suddenly, from the far wall, a cat with will power obviously weaker than his companions jumped into the arena and began gorging on the discarded crabs. This was too much for the others. Silently they joined the first, little realising the drop was easy but the return journey impossible. Soon a dozen animals were having an alfresco feast, oblivious to the trap they were in. The gang were fascinated, knowing full well the outcome when realisation dawned on both Uncle Ted and the cats.

They did not have long to wait. The back door sneaked open. There was a roaring oath and Uncle Ted charged the cats — wielding the crab scoop and kicking in all directions.

Crab meat is slippery. Crab meat and salt water are lethal. Ted was heavy and awkward. Ted's backside and the ground met forcefully. The cats scattered; flinging themselves at the wall, dropping back, running in blind panic round and round the lidless box of a yard.

'Right, you little varmints.' Ted cursed, using one of his more moderate swear words. 'You've asked for this.'

He staggered to his feet with squashed crab clinging to his trousers. The cats continued their circuit of the yard even more desperately as the fish shop fiend's eyes bulged from their sockets in anticipation of an orgy of cataclysmic proportions.

With the crab scoop held high, he advanced across the yard. Passing the bubbling pot, he glanced down and saw a cowering ginger tom endeavouring to hide under the hot cauldron. Ted let out a triumphant yell, swung once again and, with legs flailing, kicked the pot over and extinguished the gas ring.

The boiling crabs washed from the pot and swilled out

in a steaming pink flood of irresistible food. His reason snapped. He became a man possessed.

The cats were demented — torn between an overwhelming desire to eat and an over-riding instinct to avoid terrible Ted and his maiming crab scoop.

Their dilemma was solved in the shape of Aunty Ida who, hearing the commotion, opened the rear door to enquire further. 'Ted love, what . . . ?' She didn't finish the sentence but screamed as the furry, panicking cats flung themselves past her and, scuttling through the shop, made good their escape into the street beyond.

Uncle Ted sat in the disaster area surrounded by crabs and quietly sobbing.

'Never mind, love,' Antie Ida soothed, patting his back and stroking his salty hair. 'There will be other days — and it can't get any worse.'

Uncle Ted sighed heavily, slowly reached into his pocket and took out a packet of cigarettes. He fumbled with the box of matches, finally lit one and was overcome by oblivion as the gas ring exploded.

Edie's Day Off

Margaret Foreman

She tried to get the comb through her hair. At the back of her neck, her strokes met some resistance, it was a bit of a bird's nest just there.

She'd hoped to have it in good order for today. It was her day off and last month, when she'd gone home, her mother had noticed her scratching.

He mother had found the black tooth-comb from behind the mirror and combed until Edie was mesmerised, feeling a prickly crown thrilling her scalp. Then she'd had to wash it in vinegar and been told to get her comb right through it in future.

But Edie'd had little time to look to her toilet since she'd started in service as a kitchen-maid two months before. She was at cook's beck and call from rising at six until she fell exhausted into her attic bed at ten after the dinner washing-up was done. Before sleep took her though, she made time to ask her maker for help to do well in her job, so that her mother would be pleased with her.

She was thirteen and the eldest of six, though only five really, since Grace died as a baby. All the younger ones were now dispatched daily to the village school on the estate two miles away, and her mother, tall and handsome-featured, was able at last to lift her eyes from her chores for an hour or two in the middle of the day.

Edie had walked the three miles home on her first day off, but this time cook had offered the use of her bicycle as long as Edie took good care of it and didn't go through the wood, in case of punctures. Her mother would be pleased to see her home so early.

She rolled up her washing, tied it to the carrier on the

bike, and set off. The gravel on the drive crunched under her wheels as she swerved left through the small white gate and onto the path.

The day was almost balmy with just a small edgy wind to remind her that it was still only March. She began to pull the air deeply to the bottom of her lungs and push it out again, something she had forgotten how to do in that great house.

Perhaps her mother would have her new petticoat ready for her today and she could almost smell the pig's chap for tea. A jolt in a dried furrow brought her thoughts back to her ride. There was a swift tug on her long black skirt as it almost caught in the back wheel. Cook's dress-guard had unravelled and Edie would offer to re-thread it, a way of thanking her for the loan of the bike.

A downhill turn towards the stream, the air clean and clear on her face and the sight of the cottage chimney. The warmth and comfort of her family was waiting for her and encouraged her to press on strongly towards the copse on top of the next rise.

Although it was near her home, she had never felt comfortable up there. The ice-house under the lowering trees was almost buried; disused since the old squire had died. She had never played house in its murky depths with the other children, preferring the openness of the stream and fields beyond.

Closer, she could hear muffled laughter coming from the trees — probably the neighbours' little ones.

'Yoohoo,' she called to whoever was there.

A few moments later, a man's figure rose from the ice-house door. She recognised the baker who came from the town once a week. He turned quickly without acknowledging her to someone behind him, equally tall and dark. It was her mother, looking flushed and untidy.

'Oo, Edie. You are early,' she said, tidying her blouse at the waist. 'Have you been there long?'

'Cook lent me her bike,' she said. 'What's down there?'

'I thought my dog had got out of the cart and gone in there after rabbits,' said the baker.

'Well, come on Edie,' said Mother, 'Good-day, Mr Shaw — and thank you very much.'

He looked sharply at Edie then went quickly down the lane to his cart, turned to look again and then set his horse off at a smart trot. In the back of the cart the dog barked, woken by the sudden lurch forward.

On the table in the kitchen were half a dozen currant tea-cakes. Edie touched one, hoping it was still warm from the oven, but it felt cold, clammy almost.

'You haven't made these, Mam.'

'No love, I didn't. I got them from Mr Shaw.'

'I don't like him Mam — I don't know why.'

'Well, he's a kind hearted sort. He gave me the tea-cakes but don't tell your dad will you? He wouldn't eat them if he thought they were shop bought.'

Her mother didn't seem to notice Edie scratching that day and Edie didn't think to ask about her petticoat.

Right Back Where I Started From

Ian Clayton

Coming from Featherstone, as I do, carries with it certain responsibilities. Not the least of which is the necessity to explain where you're going and for how long if you're seen walking down Station Lane with a rucksack on your back. And that's exactly what happened this particular morning. Heather and me were rushing down to catch the one-fifty from the stop outside the police station when I heard the shout.

'Oy up! Where's tha' going?'

'California,' I shouted back. 'San Francisco.'

'What! On the chuffing Wakefield bus?'

That's exactly the sort of reaction you would come to expect living in Feath. Just like the time when Bert, a mate of mine, did a five-week tour of Europe on his motorbike, taking in France, Germany, Austria and Yugoslavia. He arrived back and was telling an old workmate about his adventures and finished breathless after the trek across Europe to be told — 'It's all right, cock but tha' missed a great turn down at Girnhill Lane Club t'other Saturday night.'

On the way to Wakefield we met a waiter from the local curry house who told us he'd spent some time in America and that his diabetes had started in Istanbul.

Outside Wakefield railway station a man was selling a yard of elastoplast for ten bob. Then, on the train down to London, there was a man in a shiny tinfoil suit looking for his own reserved seat when there were at least twenty seven others available . . . turkey! I leafed through a tabloid paper somebody had left behind. There was a story about a man holding up a Building Society with a cucumber in a black bin bag which he later ate on a sandwich.

I had a cup of Intercity Real Leaf Tea and it cost forty-five pence. You could get two feet seven inches of sticking plaster for that back in Wakefield.

Gatwick airport is full of disembodied voices telling you to 'Mind the doors,' 'This is the shuttle to the satellite' and 'Have a nice flight.' Then you sit on your aeroplane for at least six hours while they repair it.

So it was, that, bleary-eyed, we stepped off the plane at Minneapolis. We'd missed the flight on to San Francisco and were informed that we were to spend the night at the Comfort Inn. By then everybody was tired and frustrated, so in order to placate us, we were offered a thirteen dollar *attitude adjustment ticket* to use for dinner or breakfast. Very nice.

At the Customs I offered my best smile when they asked if I had anything to declare. 'Two jars of orange marmalade, a packet of Yorkshire tea and some shortbread biscuits.'

They put us into a motel room with the biggest double bed I've ever laid on and Heather spent ages twiddling the knob on the telly through twenty-nine different channels. Hulk Hogan laid down a wrestling challenge to Rick Funk in the *I Quit* series. Tony Bennett was singing at the re-opening of the Bay Bridge and a sleazebag show that seemed to be all cheap sex and invading aliens announced that there were thirty-five thousand weddings and five thousand divorces in Reno last year.

It still didn't feel like America until the Pizza man arrived at the door and sang a ditty praising the delights of his company's fast food. Then I knew I'd arrived.

Later, as I was washing my feet in the hand basin, I got to thinking. I wondered if Christopher Columbus felt like this the first time he rolled up a trouser leg to dip a toe in the icy waters.

Minneapolis was freezing at six o'clock the next morning and a one-armed porter was opening the front door to let the cold air in and people out. I imagine he'd have a bit of bother helping them with their luggage.

Back at the airport for the flight on to sunny California, I overheard a woman say, 'Of course the female is far superior to the male.' I bent my head over to earwig and what a tosser she was. She was talking about fur coats.

On the plane the stewardess came up to serve breakfast over the Black Hills of Dakota and asked if I wanted Wheaties. If only she knew how preposterous *'Would you like Weedees?'* sounded coming from the lips of a perfectly normal and sophisticated woman. Anyhow, I had scrambled eggs and looked down onto the Bonneville Salt Flats. Bert would have loved to ride his motorbike along there.

We landed at San Francisco and I dived through a pack of pushy-shovey Californians, all three foot taller than me, to get my rucksack from the carousel.

And here we are then — open up your Golden Gate!

Our friend Kendall lives in Haight Ashbury, once the Hippie centre of the universe, now a tourist attraction. But isn't that just what we're here for — and the Golden Gate Park is lovely.

Purston Park, near Featherstone, has only got a small boating lake and a few swings. This one has got trees from all over the world, policemen on small horses, guitar strummers strumming, old bummers bumming and the volley ball players have a whale of a time. There's a chap with the world's biggest Angora rabbit which he carries over his shoulder like a jumper. And a squirrel man in the Japanese Tea Garden who makes noises which attract squirrels into his pockets.

The Japanese Tea Garden is beautiful; full of pigeons and ducks and fish and crocodiles of children holding hands two by two. You can have jasmine tea and fortune cookies and look at the pond. A shiny blue starling came to eat cookie crumbles and a squirrel ran past with a nut in its mouth. A nutty old woman from Philadelphia cracked open her fortune cookie and announced to anybody within earshot — 'You will never know hunger.' A Mallard quacked past, laughing at her. People always throw coins in ponds like this, somebody had even thrown some into the toilet bowl.

My old gran would love it here, she only ever went to Blackpool for her holidays. In forty-nine years of marriage her and my grandad never missed once. They used to stay at Mrs Calloway's near the North Pier and they even had a box at the theatre. They visited the circus Wednesday evenings and my grandad walked on the beach every morning, and at ten to eleven ate three oysters before going for a pint of beer. They always visited the Fleetwood Market by tram and they'd spend hours watching the laughing man at the entrance to the Pleasure Beach.

Kendall's gran lives in Laguna Honda. She is ninety-four and a beautiful old Irish woman with twinkly eyes and is constantly being pestered by telephone salesmen. Beautiful ninety-four-year-old Irish women with twinkly eyes shouldn't have to put up with that. She is very sad because Kendall's mother died recently of lung cancer. Everybody said she smoked too much. Kendall's dad is still grieving too, he gets drunk and curses all the time ' . . . goddamn sonofabitch bullshit.'

My grandad died of lung cancer as well. He smoked Woodbines most of his life and worked down the pit for forty odd years. He had the biggest hands I've ever seen — just like shovels. By hell, he was a hard man. When he set his jaw he'd frighten you to death. And he was proud. I visited him in the Infirmary on the evening he died. He lay in his hospital bed, a complete wreck, weighing about six stone. He looked like a man with skeleton outside his body.

The nurses had left his tea on a tray but he hadn't touched it. I tried to feed him with Day-Glo pink blancmange from a little teaspoon, but even then he was defiant. He couldn't move his arms to stop or hit me, but he kept spitting the blancmange out — just letting it dribble out of the corner of his mouth as though to say, 'You're not bloody feeding me.'

We were invited to Kendall's dad's place for dinner one evening to eat chipino clams, mixed seafood all cooked in their shells. And afterwards, when I went into the garden for a smoke, Kendall said they used to have turtles in their pond. Then one day a racoon came and ate them all. They came out to look at the turtles and all they found were the empty shells.

One bright Sunday morning, we set out for Alcatraz Island to visit the old prison. We went by cable car from outside the world's biggest Woolworth's stores where a young mother was begging for coins and feeding her child on M & Ms. The youngster was sucking at the shells to get at the chocolate in the middle and an old busker nearby was singing Your Cheatin' Heart.

You get fantastic views of San Francisco from the cable cars and from the ferry over to the island. Once there, Ranger Mary was in charge of our party and spoke for forty-five minutes on the history, geography and botany (including where to find every porta-potty) of the island — and never once lost her smile. I bet they didn't have people like Ranger Mary when Al Capone and Machine Gun Kelly were here.

On the way back, we had Irish coffees in the Buena Vista — 'Home of the Original American Irish coffee.'

Back in the Golden Gate Park, some punks were giving out free clothes and some pushers were trying to sell barbiturates. There's plenty of drugs around — even Kendall's dad has got a joint of hashish in his sock drawer. When her mother became incurably ill, a mechanic gave them some hashish to calm their nerves. Kendall's dad is still grieving and likes to spray his wife's perfume onto the pillows every night after he's watched the ball game on telly.

After Grandad died, sometimes I forgot. Following every Featherstone Rovers match, home or away, I used to go down and give him my report on the game. So it happened that one Sunday I was well down Station Lane before I realised what I was doing. I carried on anyhow, and when I got to Gran's I told her about forgetting Grandad was dead. She said she sometimes forgot as well and remembering would start her off crying. I'd often heard her sobbing over the sink after he'd come home drunk again — and she's wept a lot since he went. But I've never heard her cry as loudly as the night the police came to tell her that he'd died.

On Telegraph Avenue, a Japanese woman was writhing about in the gutter shouting 'robbers' and 'rapists' at the top of her voice. A big fat copper from the San Francisco Police Department was sat on top of her trying to hand-cuff her. Everybody was standing around watching but nobody appeared to have seen anything. By the time the police car took her away, everybody was back to their business.

We had eggs rancheros with red beans and rice for breakfast and strolled around the Mission area watching pot-bellied little Mexican kids kicking oranges into the gutter. Kendall's bright yellow Cadillac looked a bit conspicuous there. Especially outside a rough old Mexican bar where we drank Margaritas and Richie Valens and Celia Cruz serenaded us from a battered old chrome jukebox, and a bashful giggly girl behind the bar said 'Hola' to all the old men licking salt and lemon from their hands.

I went straight up to my local when I got back and took the landlord and landlady a bottle of Californian beer apiece. The Railway Hotel has got a satellite telly now. I was just in time to see Hulk Hogan throw down a challenge in the *I Quit* series, Tony Bennett singing the praises of the Bay Bridge and the announcement that there were five thousand divorces in Reno, Nevada, last year.

Son And Idge

Tony Gaughan

They seemed to open their eyes at exactly the same instant, and then freeze, facing one another. Jaundiced light seeped through thin cotton curtains. Close to him in the double bed, Johnny could almost taste his dad's pungent sweat.

Narrowing his eyes, Greerson was the first to speak. 'What're you doing?' he asked, sitting up, the sheets tenting his raised knees. Johnny blinked, distressed and calculating, 'Go on,' his dad added before he could reply. 'Back to your own bedroom. Go on.'

Throughout breakfast a couple of hours later, Johnny was haunted by the incident. Seated opposite him, hunched over the pine table, his dad ladled sodden cornflakes into his mouth. Their eyes convened but neither of them spoke. Johnny wondered whether it had really happened. He did not dare mention it in case it had been a dream.

A little after nine and in a rush as usual, they left the house via the integral garage. The Mercedes' wheels spat a volley of gravel as they accelerated down the short drive.

The journey was spent in silence until Johnny, pointing a finger at the elaborate dashboard, said, 'If I press that switch, will we crash?'

'Don't be daft,' his dad replied.

They drove alongside chequered fields of rhubarb and rapeseed. An abandoned colliery, stark and grey, dominated the horizon.

'Will we, though?' Johnny persisted.

'Will we what?'

'Crash?'

'No.'

He pointed at another switch. 'What about that one?'

'That's the hazard lights.'

'What about that one next to it?'

'What about it?'

'If I press it, will we crash?'

'Will we hell, stupid!'

Greerson trawled plump fingers through his grey-flecked hair and glanced in the rear-view mirror. Johnny slumped back in his seat.

'Greerson and Gemidge — Quality Used Cars' was a moderately sized garage on the main dual carriageway connecting Wakefield with Leeds. The sign arching above the entrance was rickety and recently vandalised. It read 'Greer and Gem.'

'United fans,' Bob Gemmidge had said at the time.

'Somebody up there doesn't like us,' Greerson had added.

The mood was desolate until Johnny — fired by his dad's comment — suggested that the sign had been stolen by rival garage owners 'Son and Idge.' Bob had rocked with laughter and still spoke, when business was bleak, of 'those bastards Son and Idge milking us dry.'

The replacement sign had yet to arrive. Johnny could see the vandalised one through passing shutters of traffic. The car shunted forward suddenly, seizing at a gap in the wake of a double-decker bus and came to a rest in front of the office — actually a Portakabin supported by slabs of breeze block.

Johnny followed his dad into the rectangular room, beige-painted, with two desks, steel filing cabinets and the micro-computer used to store details for the finance and credit brokers. Bob Gemidge looked up over the top of his tabloid. 'Glad you could make it,' he said drily.

Greerson snatched up the electric kettle from its resting place on top of one of the filing cabinets. He weighed it in his hand and plugged it into the wall socket.

Bob shook his paper. 'Bloke in here wrapped his motor round a lamp-post and walked away,' he said.

Greerson shrugged.

'Just goes to show,' Bob added.

Johnny unhooked his overalls from the back of the office door and thrust his limbs through baggy wads of material. He was engulfed, despite alterations, in the dirty blue fabric.

He found Nick the labourer, seated on the ground behind a white Sierra, his back resting against its plastic bumper, a cigarette in his mouth. Johnny sat down beside him. He loved the way Nick smoked, his long fingers extended, the rhythmic inhalations. He nurtured a theory that it made him more intelligent, a necessary antidote to the constant accusations of stupidity levelled at him by Bob and Johnny's dad.

'You alright then?' Nick asked. Johnny nodded. Nick stood up, dusted the seat of his overalls and ground the stub of his cigarette under his boot. 'Better do some work,' he murmured.

Johnny followed him across the forecourt, past neatly parked aisles of cars, towards the workshop, a building large enough to house four cars.

Dean, the younger of the two mechanics employed by Greerson and Gemidge, was singing in accompaniment to Radio One, but twisting the lyrics — a gift of dubious distinction — so that they were either funny or obscene. He glanced up from the open bonnet of a Renault and nodded secretively at Fred as Johnny entered through the wide open doors.

Fred, working at his bench on a component, sniggered to himself. Old enough to retire, engine oil blacking the creases of his face, he seldom spoke but when he did it was invariably a joke. It was as though he had a fading reputation as a comedian and was anxious not to let it sink any further.

'Management spy's here again,' he shouted, and accompanied the comment with a parody of fevered work, hastily fastening screws, pausing to mop his brow.

Johnny ignored him with ostentation. As the boss's son, he tried to treat the mechanics with as much contempt as he could muster; not realising that this in itself was a reason for their repeated teasing.

Hands in his pockets Johnny meandered across the concrete floor, past an engine resting on a pallet, by a lathe and an ignition tuning machine. In the corner, its breeze block walls smothered with pin-ups, his mam's car, a wrecked 205, was awaiting assessment by a representative of the insurance company. All down one side and across the bonnet, the two-year-old vehicle was dented and buckled. The driver's door was so badly damaged, it would not open. Johnny clambered in through the passenger side, shuffling over the gearstick, taking the wheel in both hands. Tiny cubes of glass littered the carpeted floor. There was a dark stain on the grey upholstery.

Johnny tried to think of his mam — as she looked when she was younger — because, well, because she seemed to have aged a great deal in the last month. He thought about her clothes and her tone of voice; her hair and her laughter. She was like a ghost or a dream — not quite solid, hovering just beyond his reach. Once he'd cried in the car, but now he never cried at all. Oddly guilty, holding his breath, he hurried out of the car and the workshop into the bright August sunshine.

His dad and Bob were hunched over their desks in the office, comparing columns of figures.

'ENW 441Y,' Bob said.

'Reduced to two-two-seven-fifty,' his dad replied.

Johnny coughed. 'I'm off to the shop,' he said.

He was told as usual to cross at the traffic lights, but as usual he disregarded the advice, tearing across all four carriageways with their hurtling HGVs. There was a sense of achievement, of being cleansed, at reaching the opposite pavement intact.

He bought a Mars bar and a sherbet dip from the lugubrious Asian who ran the corner shop. Then, instead of returning directly to the garage, he made a short detour to the nearest telephone booth. He dialled the number of the garage, waited for the receiver to be lifted at the other end — and then smashed his down. In all, he did this three times. He had done it before. He did it nearly every day. He had heard Bob and his dad discussing the matter. Bob had phoned Telecom to complain. His dad blamed it on the run of bad luck they were experiencing.

Once, in a lighter mood, Bob had blamed 'Those buggers at Son and Idge,' winking as he did so at Johnny. Johnny felt the comment deserved more hilarity than it had actually received, and compensated by imagining Bob say it again, every time he played his little trick.

'Where've you been?' his dad asked on his return.

'Shop,' Johnny replied.

His dad's eyes communed with Bob's. Bob flicked through the pages of a leaflet. The silence became so intense that Johnny could hear the feeble drone of the fluorescent light. When he unwrapped his Mars bar, the covering crackled like a firework. Standing up, Bob said he was going to the fish and chip shop. Greerson gave him an order for two times.

'Which shop did you go to?' his dad said, now they were alone.

'Paki,' Johnny said.

'Where else did you go?'

'Nowhere.'

'Are you sure?'

Johnny nodded.

'You didn't go near a telephone box, did you?'

Johnny shook his head.

Greerson pursed his lips. 'If I find out you're lying . . .'

he murmured, leaving the sentence incomplete.

Lunch consisted of fish and chips eaten off greasepaper and accompanied by mugs of sweet tea. Afterwards, he was told to take his overalls off; they had to go out on business.

They joined the M62, driving through the web of newly built industrial estates swathing the southern tip of Leeds. As they drew level with enormous long vehicles, their eight or more wheels towering above the low-slung car, Johnny was tantalised by the opportunities for disaster. One loss of attention, one miscalculation or deliberately stupid manoeuvre would mean certain death.

He saw his own face with the eyes dangling from their sockets, he saw his limbs torn and seeping blood, he saw himself broken and disfigured, thronged with wires and drip tubes.

The auction, or block as his dad called it, was part of a large complex on the fringes of Huddersfield. Greerson parked his car at the foot of a low, whitewashed wall and activated the central locking with his remote control. Johnny narrowed his eyes against the sun's glare.

The auction room was like an enormous garage with doors at both ends. A procession of cars went in at one side and came out of the other. Potential purchasers pored over them, opening the bonnets, kicking the sills. Thousands of them milled about in frantic disorder. Sweat mingled with the odour of exhaust fumes. From behind his raised podium the auctioneer chanted relentlessly.

'Two-two-six? Do I have two-two-six? Two-two-six. I have two-two-six. Two-two-seven? Two-two-seven? Two-two-seven. Do I hear two-two-eight? Two-two-eight? I'm looking for two-two-eight. No. Two-two-seven then. Two-two-seven. Going at two-two-seven. Going at two-two-seven. Going. Gone.'

Johnny strained to see beyond the backs of the men surrounding him. The never-ending chant was beginning to bore him. He watched his dad, the smile of private pleasure, the way he raised one hand limply above his head as though a great deal of energy was being compressed into a minimum of physical effort.

'Sold to Greerson,' the auctioneer said. Johnny grinned, thrilled at hearing his name spoken aloud.

Greerson made four more bids and abandoned another three. Before they set off back to the garage, he told Johnny to wait outside the auctioneer's office with keen instructions not to stray, while he attended to the paperwork. Johnny did as he was told, scrutinising the hard faces of the men who circulated about him.

Son and Idge had to be there. Among all those men in their grease stains and tattoos — there had to be a Son and Idge.

'Right. Home,' his dad said, emerging from the auctioneer's office, duplicate invoices fluttering in his hand.

The M62 was choked with rush hour traffic. Heat haze rippled the tarmac; cars on the horizon shimmered like a furling flag and disappeared. Chrome and glass glinted.

Squinting, lowering his sunvisor, Greerson tapped the number of the garage into the carphone.

'Bob? It's me.' He had to shout above the din of speeding traffic. 'Yeah, yeah. I got the BMW . . . What? No. listen, Bob, you can handle that end, can't you, I've got to get off home.'

He glanced at Johnny and then back at the road. The speedo registered a steady seventy-five.

'For fuck's sake,' he added in a rush, 'you know the situation, Bob.'

He slammed the phone down and searched through a compartment for a cassette. Shirley Bassey drowned the motorway with Big Spender.

The microwave pinged downstairs while Johnny was drying himself on an off-white bath-towel which had an odour reminiscent of tallow.

'Dinner's ready,' his dad shouted up the stairs.

Zip undone, shirt hanging out, hair uncombed, Johnny entered the kitchen to be greeted by the thin scent of curry spices. Greerson was reading the back of a food carton, hunched over one of the work surfaces with a half-inch butt in his mouth. Coughing, he swivelled round.

'Seen the state of you?' he said.

It felt as though entire sections of his scalp were being removed as his dad tugged the comb through his knotted, still damp hair. He yanked at his son's flies and stuffed the shirt down the seat of his trousers.

'Bleeding useless, you are,' he muttered, 'Can't even dress yourself. How old are you? Ten or two?'

'Get off!' Johnny protested. 'You're hurting me!'

'Stand bloody still then!'

'Ow! Ow! Ow!'

'You're nowt but a pain in the arse. You hear me? The sooner you're back at school, the better.'

With a stern push, he was propelled towards the table. Lodging himself on the tip of a chair, he poked a fork at his microwave-ready Chicken Tikka.

Opposite him, his dad ate slowly, scooping saffron shaded rice from the surface of his paper plate. Belching, he scraped the debris, plate and all, into the pedal bin.

Johnny had barely touched his.

'Don't you want that?' his dad asked.

'I'm not hungry.'

'That's because you eat sweets all day.' He reached over the table and snatched Johnny's plate up. 'And don't you dare start giving it 'I'm hungry' at the hospital.'

'I don't want to go anyway,' Johnny murmured.

'You what?'

'I don't want to go.'

'You don't want to see your mother? Is that what you're saying?'

Johnny fixed his eyes on the table-top. 'What's she care anyway?' he said.

His head slipped forward under the impetus of the blow. 'She's your mother,' his dad said. 'Don't you bloody well forget that.'

Johnny nodded, embarrassed and upset, immured in strange conflicts; ashamed and angry; raging inside with the inexpressible.

The hospital was reached via the inner-city motorway and a plethora of congested minor roads. Finding a parking place frayed Greerson's patience. He tugged Johnny behind him through the hospital grounds, down utilitarian corridors, up flights of concrete stairs.

The small private room smelt of pine disinfectant. There was a vase of carnations and an untouched bowl of fruit beside the bed. Johnny's mam was linked via a plasma drip to an upturned bottle of saline solution. A multiplicity of wires connected her wrists, neck and forehead to a rhythmically blipping machine. Her face was ashen, the eyes closed, her dark hair scooped back beneath a cap of clinging lotus-green rubber.

Johnny and his dad ensconced themselves on the moulded plastic seats, one at each side of the steel-railed bed. Leant forward over the unruffled sheets, Greerson spoke softly into his wife's ear.

Not listening — not wanting to listen — Johnny watched his mam's chest deflate as she exhaled air. There was, on each of these occasions, a tantalising moment, a brief death, before the life support machine triggered a further inhalation. The slow rhythm fascinated the boy. He found himself breathing in time with the recumbent figure.

'Johnny.' His dad's anguish-stricken eyes gazed across the bed at him. 'I think you should have a word now,' he added.

Although he had long since given up all hope of resuscitating his mam by talking to her, Johnny still had to go through the motions. It was a task he could not escape from. The doctors demanded it. His dad demanded it. We have to let her know that she's not alone. That's what his dad had said. That's what the doctors had told him. Johnny sometimes felt as though his words were flowers laid on a grave.

'What shall I say?' he said, looking up.

'Tell her what you've done today.'

'But I haven't done anything.'

Gritting his teeth, angry, Greerson shook his head and mouthed some stern curse.

Johnny shuffled in his seat. 'Well,' he began. 'I went to work with my dad again. Er, we went to the car auction and we had some fish and chips and . . .' A word appeared on the tip of his tongue. Fuck disappeared but cunt came to replace it. 'And it was really sunny and . . .' He felt like laughing. Cunt, Fuck, Son and Idge. '. . . and it was good fun really.' Son and Idge. Cock. Tits. 'I saw your car again. My dad's going to mend it for when you're better.' Wake up. Why wouldn't she wake up? 'That's about it really.'

He glanced at his dad. 'I can't think of anything else,' he said.

'Okay.' He rubbed the tip of his little finger, the flesh browned with nicotine, in the corner of an eye. He stood up. 'It's been a long day, love,' he said apologetically.

The machine blipped with the regularity of a metronome. Johnny, also standing, stared down at his mam. There were times when her stony silence seemed to scream, reach a crescendo of frustration.

They listened to the radio during the long drive home.

It was still light when Greerson parked the car in front of the garage. Under normal circumstances he would have put it away for the night.

'Are you going to the pub?' Johnny asked.

Greerson rubbed his nose, the car keys jangling in his hand. 'I don't know,' he said.

The sky was scuffed with cirrus, lit orange and red on the horizons. The scent of rapeseed, dry and sensual, drifted over from the nearby fields. Johnny followed his dad into the kitchen and the fluorescent tube stuttered to life.

Lighting a cigarette, Greerson said, 'When you're older, we'll be able to go to the pub together.'

'You are going then?' Johnny said.

'You don't mind, do you? A big lad like you.'

Johnny didn't reply. He headed down the hallway into the lounge. Scatter cushions were strewn on the couch. Horse brasses hung from the artificial beams embedded in the ceiling. Johnny switched on the television and sat down on the carpet in front of it.

His dad had appeared in the doorway. 'I'll be over at The Nook,' he said. 'Put something in the microwave if you get hungry.'

He waited until his dad's car had joined the erratic stream of traffic at the foot of the drive before making his way upstairs. He drifted aimlessly from room to room. The toys in his bedroom failed to interest him. Plastic fighter planes were suspended on thread from the ceiling. Guns and robots and unidentifiable constructs of Lego overflowed the lid of his toy chest. He had outgrown it all. He was too old to play. The entire house seemed to belong to someone else. Someone young and foolish. The person he used to be.

A sound on the landing caught his attention. 'Who is it?' he said.

Stealthy now, he searched one bedroom after the other. He searched them twice in case he'd missed something.

'Son and Idge,' he said with sudden realisation.

On the landing, nestling aginst the skirting board, he discovered a large, hairy spider. Excited, he ran to fetch a glass from the bathroom and trapped the creature beneath it. When it climbed up the walls of the glass, he cut off its only escape route by sliding a paperback beneath the circular rim. He stared at this prize proudly.

'Prepare to die,' he said.

Descending to the kitchen, he swung open the door to the microwave and let the creature clamber loose. It was trapped again when he closed the door. There were nine power levels and Johnny chose the highest. He set the timer at three minutes. The internal light came on when he pressed 'Cook'.

The turntable began to spin round. Immediately, the spider reacted. It flexed its legs as the hairs on its back began to melt. Once flexed, the legs snapped and sizzled away from beneath it. The fat body fell pulsating on the opaque glass of the turntable. Waves rippled on its steaming skin. The skin cracked and black boiling stuff oozed through the fracture. Within seconds there was nothing left of it but a smear of ash. The timer pinged and the internal light switched itself off.

Goose pimples granulated Johnny's skin. He felt himself tremble. He felt ill. Perhaps it was the fumes from the atomised spider. Perhaps it was the rapidly falling darkness and the temperature reduction in its wake. The living room, when he entered, seemed chill and foreboding. The ceiling looked oddly angled at one edge. The room seemed longer, stretched along its axis. And hadn't the settee been drawn nearer the unlit fire?

A wave of panic passed over him. He sat down at the telephone table and caressed the handset. After a moment he punched out the number of the garage.

'*Thank you for your phone call,*' his dad's voice said. '*Unfortunately, the staff at Greerson and Gemidge's are unavailable at the moment. If you'd care to leave your name and number after the tone, we'll get back to you as soon as possible.*'

Johnny blew a raspberry and crashed down the receiver. A moment later, he dialled the same number. The message repeated itself, the same forced cadences, the gruff Northern edges smoothed away; a different way of talking for a different situation — like when he talked to his mam, Johnny thought.

'Son and Idge here,' Johnny said, breaking into a giggle. He replaced the receiver and snatched it up again. Again the same message. Again his dad's incorporeal voice. Is this how it must seem to his mam? Familiar voices exuding from the dark, not quite sincere, not quite normal.

'This is Son and Idge. We're coming to get you. You're dead.' The receiver slipped from his hand as he staggered back. The room, all at once, seemed to crowd in on him. 'Son and Idge, Son and Idge, Son and Idge.' He chanted as the man had chanted at the auction. Wheeling round, he snatched a cushion from the settee and threw it at the wall. A Constable print slipped sideways from its hanger. 'Son and Idge, Son and Idge, Son and Idge.'

Realisation shot through him — he had left a message on the ansaphone. Bob would hear it in the morning. He would tell his dad. 'If I found out you're lying . . .'

The onyx ashtray felt heavy in his hand. A trickle of butts teemed from it. Grimacing, he heaved it through the patio window. Shards of glass littered the stone flags outside, glittering amid the tubs of trailing lobelia and crimson flowered geraniums.

Johnny sank to his knees, realising now the full impact of his actions. Exhausted and ashamed, he cried into his cupped hands. He cried until he fell asleep.

He was aroused by the sound of his dad singing *Yesterday* in the kitchen. He sat up, his eyes gradually acclimatising to the surrounding darkness. Jumping to his feet, he tried vainly to right the damage he found all around him. His dad's footsteps approached.

'Johnny. Johnny.'

There was no escape from what was to come. He saw it amassing before his eyes, gathering shape, dark and void-like, smacking of jeopardy.

Greerson, flicking on the light switch, blinked in disbelief. 'What the . . .'

In the hundred watt glare, the true extent of the damage was revealed. His dad's eyes, glistening and confused, appealed to him across the desolation.

'Why?' he said. 'Why?'

Johnny began to sob.

'Do you hate me? Is that it?'

The tears streamed down Johnny's cheeks.

'Do you think I like this . . . this situation . . . ?' He lurched over to the sofa and sat down. His eyes fed tears into the palm of his hand. 'Oh fucking hell,' he whined. 'Oh fucking hell.'

'I want me mam,' Johnny murmured through his tears, 'I want me mam.'

'I know you do. I know you do.'

Darting forward, he enclosed his son in a tight embrace. He shook the boy gently from side to side. Johnny relaxed in the supportive hug. His eyes flickered shut. For a moment, he fell asleep. He had been led up the stairs when he came round. Everything was like a dream, even the waking. Greerson helped him into his pyjamas and supervised his entry into the single bed adorned with the continental quilt.

'Go to sleep now.'

Johnny's eyes were half-closed anyway. The pillows were soft beneath his head. He heard his dad's feet padding softly down the stairs. The night was warm and still. It wrapped itself round the boy, engulfing him in darkness.

To Be A Fisherman

Terry Wilson

As a young lad, I was fascinated by the river. Clear and sparkling, tumbling away over the rocks, fast and furious in a peaty spate. There was always something to do. Walking around the rock pools. Exploring under every ledge — every stone between the weir and the river bridge. Chasing minnows. Standing behind the waterfall. Hot, long summer days when only tiredness called you home.

That's when you'd see them come down to the river. Fishermen — fly fishermen. Casting lines of silent silk. Landing like thistledown. Sucking trout. Rings on the surface — rippling outwards. They talked amongst themselves, I was only a lad, I had to go home.

But one day I'd be older, then I'd be a real fisherman. I'd have a rod. I'd be a shadow at dusk. I'd catch trout. Dreams — they were a long way off. I'd have to learn, but I knew where they were. Every run, every trickle, every mood. I knew where they liked to be. I watched some nights from the bridge — when the fishermen thought I'd gone. Some were good, some hadn't a clue. One day I'd show them where the real trout lurked.

It was fun and furtive, tickling trout. It could only be done in summer days when you could stand knee deep in the pools or lay on the rocks and lean over the edges. I had to pretend it was only minnows and bullheads I was after. The trout were for the fishermen. But the odd one was quickly slipped inside my shirt and a fast scurry back home. Mostly I let them go. I could play with them; stroking under the belly, rolling over like a dog — asking for more. They were my friends, my company. Often I saw no-one all day but I was never lonely. I did want to match wits with them though. Play them at nature.

Seemed to me there were two problems. The first was half-a-crown; I'd had one last Christmas in my stocking. Without one now I'd be in bother. Grandma was sat in the deck chair, by the dark red peonies in the front garden. A typical Grandma — warm and understanding, always an odd coin in the back of her purse. She understood. Half-a-crown for a licence was vital. I wanted to be a fisherman but I didn't want to get into bother.

I watched Sid Clark at the ironmonger's fill in my name and address on the yellow licence. He kept peering down at me over the counter, muttering. He gave it to me. I had a last look at the only two and sixpence I'd see between now and next Christmas and handed it over. I was now a fisherman, it was official. The Licence said so.

I looked at his rods, reels and lines in the window. Problem number two — or two, three and four.

We had canes at home, some long ones for the sweet peas. We had bobbins for sewing. We had string — green — like the fly fisherman's line. We had wire — I could make rings for the rod. I'd saved bits of nylon and a few rusty hooks found in the bushes by the river. An odd float too. I could make flies from Uncle Tom's hen feathers.

It was a proud moment when at last I stood by my favourite pool. The challenge was on as I flicked the float under the bushes where the current runs in. It was a lovely evening. At peace with the world.

'What do you think you're up to?'

It made me jump. I turned. It was a fat, ruddy-faced man wearing one of those hats that go forwards and backwards, full of fishing flies.

'Fishing, mister.'

'You need a licence to fish.'

I proudly reached inside my jerkin pocket and pulled it out.

'That's me — Terry Wilson.'

'I know who you are — you're always hanging about t'river. Now clear off.'

'But mister, I've got a licence.'

'Doesn't matter. You've not got permission. You can't fish here.'

'But it cost me half-a-crown mister. Where can I fish please?'

'Nowhere — it's all ours — it's Haythorne Angling Club.'

'All of it?'

'Aye, all of it. Six miles upstream and six miles down — now clear off.'

I was sad walking back home, over the bridge. Three fellers made a joke about my tackle as I went around the corner.

The river couldn't be *all* theirs — not *all* of it. There was a club, I knew that. Mr Catlow, who ran the picture house, was in charge. He was nice. But all the people seemed well-off who were members, beyond the hope of lads like me. Even if I had the money, they'd not let me join. They kept it posh.

It was a problem.

Saturday nights, Grandma and Mrs Fell always went to the pictures, end seats in the bottom half. Would she ask Mr Catlow about it for me?

'There you are, Terry,' Grandma said as she came back in from the pictures. 'Mr Catlow has sent you last year's rule book — says they've had all that fishing for years. It gives the names of all the members, a big waiting list to get in, mostly business people. Even then, it costs five pounds to join. I'm sorry, love.'

I took the yellow rule book upstairs. A folding map fell out. It showed all the river from Wainsforth to Ington. All the Angling Club owned was marked in black. I pored over it. It was nearly all black. But wait! — there seemed to be the odd small gap — why, why?

I was about to invent the Terry Wilson Fishing Club, membership restricted to one. But there were a few people I'd got to go and see first. Mr Frankland — he owned the saw mill between the weir and river bridge. He was also the undertaker. Point in my favour here. Grandma used to lay out the folks who'd died for Mr Frankland. His saw mill bordered the river with about three feet of grassy bank but there was no way down to it. It was a blank on the fishing club map.

I found Mr Frankland in his timber yard. He listened to me and smiled sympathetically.

'So long as you promise not to fish it in a flood, we might be able to help. Follow me.'

We went under the shed with its green corrugated roof, where the ladders were kept.

'Look over this wall,' he said, and there below was the river — eight or ten feet down.

He picked up what looked like a rope ladder, but it was made of metal and wire all coiled up. It was hooked onto the wall.

'We sometimes have to get down to the river to wash the buckets out,' he said. 'Just toss the coil over the wall and climb down. Bring it up when you've done. And a nice trout would do nicely if you get a spare one sometime, Terry.'

'Thanks ever so, Mr Frankland,' I called as I skipped away. Off to the next blank on the map! — Lizzie Cox's.

Lizzie had the end cottage of six just below Mr Frankland's mill. Same problem, there was a steep drop down to the river. But more importantly, it was the last cottage before the bridge and the mill race went under all the cottage gardens and came out underneath hers.

Now Lizzie sold sweets, pop and cigs from her back room. I used to go regularly. It was time to point out to Mrs Cox that I was probably her best customer! I came back out with a bag of mixed sherbet, a big smile on my face and a key for her back gate which I had to keep safe.

Back home and a good day's work done. Time to mark my map up. I smiled as I went to sleep.

Tomorrow it would be Widdup's Paper Mill, a mile further down river. It had a twenty foot drop down to the river — but so what? — they had windows, mostly broken, and I'd only need one. It was a draughty place. Mum worked there and I helped when I'd nothing to do. By ten o'clock that morning, in exchange for a window, I had promised Mr Widdup my undying loyalty to pull his paper trucks across the yard on Saturday mornings. Another mark on my map.

Next on the list — Jimmy Dodd's car dump behind his garage. It bordered the river. Rusting junk everywhere, but marvellous for finding ball bearings to use as marbles and Castrol oil drums for rafts. Now Jimmy liked to beat the system, and having explained I was up against a monopoly I soon added another mark to my map.

And so it went on. Dot after dot went onto my map and eventually the plan went into action. I started fishing.

'What the blazes is that?' asked two old blokes looking downstream from on top of the river bridge.

A sparkling twelve-inch trout was being pulled along the surface by a little red float disappearing under the bridge and heading for Lizzie Cox's. An astonished fly fisherman below the bridge looked on in disbelief. The two old blokes scurried across the road in time to see me hauling the fish up and over Lizzie's back wall — and it was all legal as long as I stood on my own patch.

I had a dib of kali.

Suddenly I was starting to become very unpopular — with fishermen! They were mystified. Those were the evenings I'd walk home with two or three lovely trout. Conversations such as 'fishing's no good tonight, too clear,' would suddenly stop as I walked past.

Instead, all sorts of questions were asked — 'What's he carry that cow's horn for? What's in it?'

Many's the time I'd watched trout nose stones up to catch mayfly larvae. My horn was full of them.

Mayhem went on all summer as more big trout were carried home and fish were spirited up to heaven through a window of Widdup's Mill.

One January evening, Mr Catlow from the fishing club called at our house.

'Terry, we've just had our Annual General Meeting. They've asked me to invite you to join our club and no fee till you leave school, provided you follow our rules and only fish on our water.'

'Thank you, Mr Catlow.'

'Thank you, Terry,' he said, winking. 'The Committee will be very relieved.'

Knowing Eyes

Joan Thornton

Pigs. They eat like pigs. It's disgusting. I long since gave up trying to teach them different though, and now I let them get on with it. I just make sure I'm never in the kitchen while they're eating. I put their food in front of them and then go into the front room and leave them to it.

I don't know what ever I saw in Arthur Gawber. He must have had something going for him at one time, but thirty-eight years married and I've long since forgotten what it was. Happen it was because he seemed the strong silent type, with him being a miner and not having much to say for himself. Three sandwiches short of a picnic he is, but it took me a few years to work that out for myself and by then I had the two bairns.

You see, you don't stop to question, do you? He's the man of the house, you're just the little woman — general dogsbody's more like, though. So by the time you stop to wonder what's happening to your life, it's too late. And there's nothing you can do but make the best of it.

I dare say it's nothing unusual for a wife to find she no longer has any love or respect for her husband, but it's a sorry day when a mother has to admit she doesn't like her own sons. There's no helping it though, they take too much after their father.

Eric, he's the eldest, he's thirty-eight. Thirty-eight you're asking yourself? Yes, I admit it. Eric was on the way when me and Arthur got married.

'I'll do my duty by you,' he said. 'I'll marry you so the kid'll not be a bastard. But don't expect me to like it.'

Well, I was so grateful to him at the time — the shame would have killed my mother — so I didn't stop to consider.

Strong and silent did I say? A surly brute's what he really is. I don't think a day's gone by when he hasn't, one way or another, reminded me that he only wed me for the sake of the bairn.

'You shouldn't complain,' said my mother. 'At least he works regular.'

Oh yes, he works regular, though I see precious little of what he earns. And he drinks regular and he knocks me about regular. After a while though, you stop feeling anything. I mean on the outside the knocks still hurt; but on the inside you go sort of numb.

I did try. In the early years. Till I realised that you only find romance and holy wedlock together in books; in novels that've got nothing to do with real life. I suppose I can understand why so many women read them. Escapism. But not for me. I read a few. Lord knows I was looking for escape. For real, though, not for fantasy. By the time I realised there was no escape, Eric would be four, Bernie two and another on the way. I thank God that I lost it though. Lord, I was grieved enough at the time, but when I look at the two great brutes my bairns turned into, I can't but wish I hadn't carried both them to full term either.

That's when I stopped reading romances. All they did was make me weep. What with them poor innocent heroines, going into marriage all starry-eyed and lovey-dovey. Buckets I wept, but it changed nothing. So I stopped reading them novels, thinking the sooner I got daft ideas of romance out of my head the sooner I'd settle down and get on with real marriage.

I should have written and told the folk who write them books. I should have told them it's not like that and it's wrong to put such fanciful ideas in young girls' heads. But I didn't. Who'd listen? Nobody wants to hear the real truth of it. Anyway, they probably know how it is but they don't want to hear it said. Time comes soon enough when you've got to find out the harsh realities for yourself. And knowing about it in advance won't stop it happening. You think you're different and only when it's too late do you find you're not.

The cat was in a shallow hole in the long grass down behind the allotments. The whippet rooted it out. It looked as if it had just curled up there to die. Perhaps it had taken a knock from a passing car, perhaps it was just old age. Probably that. It looked sort of shabby and moth-eaten and it took a lot of cooking to tender it up. Thought it was just sleeping at first, curled up like it was, and I bent down to stroke it. Starting to stiffen up but it was still warmish so it hadn't been long dead.

I'd nothing but sixty-eight pence in my purse and on the way to the shops to see what I could get to make a meal for three strapping men after they've done a shift at the pit. So that's when I had the thought. After all, needs must when the devil drives and I'd rather make my excuses with the Maker for what I've done than face them three when they get in, with hungry bellies and no dinner to put in front of them.

I didn't feel right good about skinning and gutting it. Poor little bugger, I thought. And then I thought, well it were dead anyway, so it's not going to make any difference to the cat whether it gets eaten by humans or by worms. And I gave the giblets to the whippet.

After they'd eaten the cat and no complaints, I gave them the dog. Not all at once, mind. The cat was a bit scrawny but it made a meal for the three of them, with plenty of taties and cabbage and a drop of nice gravy. They didn't know that it wasn't a bit of rabbit.

The dog made a few meals. It was middling size, one of them long, lean, ginger-haired things. Red setters I think they're called. I hoped it would go further, but Arthur's a big man and the lads take after him. Brawny lads. Plenty of muscle but not much brain and all of them good trenchers — so the dog saw them half-way through the week. It was gone by Thursday, though, and I had to get a couple of pig hocks and some black pudding in for supper.

Course, the red setter wasn't dead when I found it, but its back end had gone. Couldn't get up, so I dragged it out of the road or the next wagon that passed and it would have been spread all over like strawberry jam. Terrible road it is. Them heavy wagons come down here at such a speed, there's always somebody's pet getting knocked down. And two kiddies there were, one back in eighty-two or three and one last winter. The nights draw in fast come November and them lorry drivers don't bother slowing down and by the time they see them it's too late. Bonny little lass, she was. Her parents were heart-broken. They got a petition up for the council to do something about it. I signed it myself, but nothing's been done.

Well, I couldn't leave poor little devil in the ditch there. It were whimpering, all pathetic like. There were nothing I could do for it, no idea who it belonged to so in the end I thought — the best thing I can do is put it out of its misery. So there were half a brick nearby and I hit it with that. The way it looked at me; them soulful eyes. I felt right bad about it. But if were for the best. And then I thought, well there's no point in wasting it. So I covered it up with a bit of old carpet that was in the ditch and then I waited till it was getting darker before I fetched the barrow from down the allotments.

Then Arthur got me a freezer. Him and the lads give me twenty pounds each out of their pay packets and out of that I'm expected to keep them and pay the rent and everything. So what they think I've got left out of that to stock a freezer with, I don't know. It were a peace offering really because he also gave me two black eyes and a broken nose; it's not made me any bonnier but it's a long time since any man ever looked at me anyway. And it's not the first time he's broken it so it weren't worth making any fuss over.

That's what's so nice about living round here. Folk mind their own business. A man can beat his wife half to death and the neighbours won't see it their place to interfere. You see a woman walking round with black eyes and they all think, well she must have asked for it, she must have done something to deserve it. So in a fit of remorse, I suppose you might call it, or to bribe me to keep my mouth shut and not report him, Arthur gets this freezer delivered and I'm expected to sound all excited and grateful about it. Mind you, I did, otherwise he'd have given me another backhander.

Being knocked about has what you might call its compensations though. That's how I got the washer, a fancy automatic and I still haven't figured out how it works because it had no instructions with it. Bernie got it for me after he'd thrown a kettle of boiling water at me. Arthur got real mad with Bernie about that. In fact they had a bit of a fight over it because Bernie marked my face quite bad.

'Sons shouldn't go hurting their mothers,' he told him. I suppose he thought that hitting me was his privilege. 'They should respect their mothers for bringing them into the world and looking after them.' And he fetched Bernie a good clout.

It was a mistake. It were all right for him to belt the lads when they were little, but now they're great hefty sods and big enought to fight back. Anyway, he forgets he's not as young as he was. So they start fighting in the scullery and Eric joins in — just for the hell of it, I suppose. Arthur got that mad he went for Bernie with the axe. I must have left it at the cellar head after I'd been down to chop a bit of kindling for the fire. Well, Bernie dodged and I got in the way so as well as putting the axe through the rollers of my mangle, Arthur also took two of my fingers off.

He said it were an accident, he didn't mean to, but the mangle was that old, there was no chance of getting new rollers for it. So Arthur made Bernie get the new washer for me, like you know, to say he was sorry. And over the years, that's more or less how I got the fridge and the double-oven cooker and the microwave and the food processor — and the scars.

They have this mate what goes in the Cross Keys who can get anything cheap. Usually a bit damaged, no instructions, no guarantee or anything — but cheap.

Well, at first I thought the freezer would be just a white elephant. It's so big it won't fit in the scullery and has to go down the cellar. Still, that's no hardship, I'm up and down there half a dozen times a day to fetch coal up. Then I got into the habit of freezing spare veg from the allotment and buying up anything that's going cheap and freezing it myself. And any cats or dogs that come a cropper on the road. They take a bit of scraping up sometimes if you don't get to them straight away.

Then, when the bull terrier from three doors down got into our yard and went for the whippet and tore his ear off, I knew I'd get a good hiding over it so I decided I'd make sure the bull terrier got his first and I took the axe to it. Nasty, ugly brute it was. Serves it right and it stocked the freezer up a bit. I gave the giblets to the whippet to cheer it up and had a go at sewing its ear back on. You could tell though, so I knew I was still going to cop it when they got home.

The three of them had gone shares buying that whippet. Thought they were going to make a fortune out of it, but it wasn't much of a runner. Probably fell off the back of the same wagon all the other stuff came off. They gave me a diet sheet for when it's in training. Fresh liver, braising steak and what have you. I don't know how the devil they expected me to buy all that out of the money they gave me for housekeeping. But neither do I argue about it, I tell them it's getting the good stuff and give it scraps and leftovers. After all, the dog's not going to tell no tales.

There's a fair number of dead birds lying around if you

know where to look, it's the local cats — too many of them, though there's less than there were. There's also plenty of rats down the allotment because of the pigeons, so they set traps for them. I go round regular and empty them. Not a nice job but some real big ones get caught, all the pigeon corn and stuff I suppose they feed on, but I've done worse jobs and there's a surprising bit of meat on them. Done in a pie or a stew, with some tasty gravy and home grown veg, who's to know what they were?

I've not eaten any of it myself but neither have I had any complaints. And the whippet never tuns his nose up at the heads and innards. In fact, he seems to be running better. He came in third down at the dog track last Wednesday, and his coat's looking shinier.

Arthur died just after Christmas. Too much, what d'you call it? — cholesterol. And beer. Came back early from the pub. Said he weren't feeling too well. Didn't stop him having a go at me because his supper weren't ready, so I nipped out of his way and tried to hide in the cellar. I grabbed the axe, just for protection mind — to stop him using it on me again. When I saw his legs coming down the cellar steps, I don't know what came over me but I went for them. I went for his feet with the axe. He'd still got his work boots on so it didn't do much damage, but it scared him enough and he tried to get out of the way when he saw me ready to take another swing.

Tripped over his own great sodding feet he did. Sprawled at the bottom of the cellar steps clutching his leg and howling. I was standing over him trying to make up my mind whether to fetch help or what. But then he stopped clutching his leg and clutched his chest. His face. Terrible look of pain he had. Went an awful colour. Sort of gasping for air. He grabbed hold of my ankle but I kicked him off. Thought it might be some sort of a trick. And then he half sits up, makes this terrible moan and falls back dead. I think he was dead but I didn't intend getting too close.

So there I was. Left with this dilemma. Do I send for the police or an ambulance — or what? He was a big man, plenty of meat on him. But then I think, well if he just disappears, it's going to take some explaining, and the police might ask some funny questions. Then again, it did seem a shame to let all that food go to waste. On the other hand — call it sentiment if you like, but butchering Arthur wasn't a job I was sure I could stomach. Not with knowing him so intimately. And it would be a big job, he would take some handling.

So I ran down to the Cross Keys and fetched the lads and they did what was necessary. I told the police he'd fallen and the autopsy said it was his heart. They asked a lot of questions to find out whether the heart attack caused the fall or the fall caused the heart attack. But with folk at the pub confirming that he left early because he wasn't feeling well, they decided the heart attack came first. And nobody asked about the slit in the top of his right boot.

With Arthur gone, I get a widow's pension, but Eric and Bernie are less reliable at handing over their twenty pounds a week and if I remind them too often, I'm likely to find myself with a thump. Eric's worse, he seems to think it's his job to take over where his dad left off.

The widow's pension is the first time I've ever had anything to call my own. Oh if only, I sometimes think, if only they'd both find themselves a nice girl to settle down with and leave home. With my pension, and maybe I could claim something towards the rent, I'd get by. Mind you, I wouldn't wish them great beasts on any of the lasses in the village, even if any showed any inclination to either of them — which they don't.

They drink even more now Arthur's not here to keep

them in line. It makes Eric even more handy with his fists, — and Bernie? Well, Bernie's the sly one.

*

Saturday it was, couple of months after we buried Arthur, they'd gone to a football match. Eric come rushing into the house all covered in blood. He wouldn't tell me what happened at first, he just grabbed a suitcase off the top of the wardrobe and starts throwing clothes in. Then he says he's leaving and asks for whatever money I've got in the house. When I told him I hadn't got any he flew into a real temper and he put them great hands round my neck. Fingers like a pound of thick sausages he has. He reeked of booze and he started squeezing my neck and he said seeing as he'd already killed a chap, killing me wouldn't make any difference.

I was half choked and could see he meant it, so I said I'd get the money. I went down the cellar. I'd got a few pounds tucked in the corner of the freezer, though I wasn't happy at parting with it. It was only twenty-two pounds, but it had taken me twice as many weeks to save it up.

He followed me down. I expected he would, so I asked him to reach into the bottom of the freezer to get to the money. It's always been a bit of a struggle to get right down to the bottom when there isn't much in it, with it being a big chest freezer and me being no more than five foot one.

So as he bent right inside, I swung the axe down hard on his neck and nearly took his head off. Then I had to work fast. If he'd killed somebody like he said, which didn't surprise me because when he gets fighting drunk it doesn't take much to set him off, it wouldn't be long before the police were at the door.

Lord, it was hard work lugging him about and hacking him up. And I was that worn out and frantic, there was no room for sentiment. I hadn't done when Bernie got in from the match, so I shoved what I could in the freezer. But the bulk of him — it was still too heavy to lift so I just pulled a sack over him and hoped for the best. After all, Bernie never has no reason to come down the cellar. He never chops any sticks or fetches a bucket of coal up.

Bernie said a fight had broken out at the match. A big fight. With a bit of luck it would be on telly, he said. Hundreds of folk tanked up with beer and ready to take on anybody. The last he'd seen of Eric he was wading into the thick of it. Bernie cleared off. He's not a real fighter — just a bully. So he didn't see what happened to Eric after that.

I told him Eric had come home and packed his things and left because he'd killed a bloke and he was on the run. I was trembling all over. I don't know how I didn't give the game away, but Bernie didn't seem to suspect. He went down to the Cross Keys and said he'd ask around, see what he could find out.

He didn't get back till turned midnight so it gave me time to finish working on Eric and clean up the mess. The whippet got a bit excitable so I gave him some scraps to quieten him and then I walked him down to the local tip with the suitcase and all Eric's clothes. I thought it best to burn them instead of just dumping them, but it's surprising how long it takes to burn a good wool suit and Eric never stinted when it came to spending on himself.

I tried to listen to the news, but I couldn't settle so I had myself a drop of Eric's whisky, he wasn't going to mind was he, and went to bed. With that and all the toil of seeing to Eric, I went out like a light.

Bernie barged into the bedroom gone midnight, drunk as a lord and stinking like a pig and flopped down on the bed.

'It's right Mam,' he said. 'A bloke got killed. He was knifed — and plenty of witnesses. If Eric's scarpered, he'd better put plenty of distance between him and here because once the cops start sniffing round, it won't be long before they're onto him. It's just you and me on our own now, Mam.'

He made a grab at me and then rolled over and fell asleep and started snoring like the pig he is. I slipped out of bed and spent the rest of the night on the settee with the whippet asleep across my feet. I was a long time dropping off again and having that whippet there gave me a bit of comfort.

The police came. They made their inquiries, listened to what I told them and took Eric's photo — the one he had taken on the fishing trip to Brid last year. It were broadcast on the telly the same night. It said they were looking for him in connection with a murder and anyone seeing him should tell the police and not approach him because he might be dangerous.

For the first few weeks, they kept coming back to see if we'd heard anything from him. I think they was watching the house in case he tried to come home. I knew they were wasting their time, but I couldn't tell them that. The hue and cry gradually died down but the police still popped round now and again. Usually it was the local community bobby and I think he just took to dropping in for a cup of tea when he'd nothing better to do. It didn't half make me nervous though. I don't reckon they ever suspected what really happened. They searched the house to see if he'd left any clues but they never looked in the freezer.

Trouble was, then I was down to my pension and whatever Bernie gave me — when he felt like it. He still troughed like a pig, almost made up for the other two, and though there was plenty of meat to go at, you need money for other things when you've got a house to run. Then the rent went up and not long after the electric bill and poll tax bill came in the same post — and that was more than I could cope with, so I'd no choice but to ask Bernie for some money.

He called me some terrible names and accused me of

squandering his money. He would never have talked to me like that if Arthur had still been alive. Said he wasn't paying no poll tax on principle — though that's got to be the first principle I've ever known him have. I suppose I'll end up paying it for him. He did give me a bit towards the electric bill but not before landing out and knocking me against the cooker edge so I split my lip and broke my top denture. My real teeth have been knocked out, a few at a time over the years, so I've dentures top and bottom and no money to get them repaired. He threw a handful of notes at me though, as he went out to the pub.

It was that same night he came to my bed. I was asleep but soon woke when he pulled the covers off me and his great fist grabbed hold of my nightie and yanked it till it tore. The light was off, it was as black as pitch but I recognised that booze and pig stink. Oh Lord, I thought, it's come to this. Then he flopped down on me and it was like being hit by a tank. About eighteen stone and it knocked all the wind out of me, so I couldn't put up much of a fight. Anyway, where's the point, I knew he'd do what he wanted whether I let him or not.

'You shouldn't do this, Bernie. I'm your mam,' I said.

'Some cats mights be scrawnier than others,' he said, 'but they're all grey in the dark.' He laughed. A vile sound it were.

'It's not right,' I said, 'I'm your mam.'

'But I'm keeping you now instead of Dad, so I'm entitled to his privileges.'

I couldn't stop him. He was heaving and grunting like the animal he is, and just like Arthur was. So I lay there and let him get on with it, and just like Arthur, a couple of minutes and he was done.

'About last night,' he says next morning. 'I were drunk.'

As if that made it all right. Anyway, it didn't stop him from getting drunk and doing it again. And whenever it suited, whether he were drunk or not. He gave me a bit more money though, and more regular. So I took it — fed him Eric in return and bided my time.

'You've only one lad left at home now, Mrs Gawber,' says Selma Packman, two doors up. 'You'll miss him if he ever meets a nice lass and gets married. All on your own you'll be then.'

'Aye,' I says, trying to sound all wistful like. 'But it's only right you bring your kids up to be independent and leave home.'

'Still, you're all right for a bit yet. Your Bernie hasn't even got a girl friend and doesn't show much inclination either.'

'Well, that's where you're wrong,' I says, swanking like, because I want her to think I know something she doesn't. 'Lives down south. He's been writing to her some time now and it's serious. He's been talking about going to see her.'

'Oh, aye,' she says, really interested.

'But I'd better not say any more. He's asked me not to tell. Our Bernie don't reckon anything to women who've got nothing better to do than gossip about other folk. So don't you go saying anything either.'

'Oh, I won't,' she says.

And I know she will.

So when Bernie took his fortnight's holiday, telling everybody he was off on a fishing trip, folk weren't that surprised afterwards when I told them he'd really gone to see this girl he'd been writing to in secret. And just when he was due back at work, I went down to the pit with a note, that looked near enough like Bernie's writing, asking for his cards and P45 as he'd got a job down south and wouldn't be coming back.

With my pension and the other benefits I can claim now I'm on my own, I get by. And Bernie's money's a bonus. Being sly and underhand himself, he didn't trust anybody else either. Or banks and building societies. I found the money in the lining of one of his old jackets at the back of the wardrobe when I was clearing out. It paid for some new teeth and a holiday.

Two weeks I spent in Torquay in a nice boarding house. I took the whippet with me because I told Selma I'd be staying with Bernie and his new wife. Said they'd got married quiet at the registry office because they didn't want any fuss.

It was a lovely holiday, first time I'd been away since I was seventeen. I even brought back a photo of a young woman standing by a gate with the whippet. Showed it to Selma Packman and said she was Bernie's wife. Friendly young woman she was, staying at the same boarding house as me. She was on her own as well, so we'd sometimes go for a walk together. The photo's too blurred to see any details clear; must have moved the camera when I was taking it.

That holiday didn't half do me good. I'm not having nearly so much trouble with my nerves now and I've got a good appetite. Of course, I never fancy anything out of the freezer — I buy fresh each day from the shops but the whippet's getting through it steady. In fact he's getting so fat he doesn't look like a whippet these days. His racing career's definitely over but I've grown real fond of that dog. He's good company and sometimes, well, the way he looks at me sometimes — them knowing eyes — well it's a good job dogs can't talk.

The Shepherd's Cottage

Hilary Shields

Shepherd's Cottage was a one-up, one-down dwelling tied to Grimwade's Farm. There was a room to live in downstairs with a latched door which opened to show the steep, narrow staircase leading up to the only bedroom. At the back of the cottage was a lean-to scullery where a yellow stone sink stood on brick legs.

Ted Gregory, following his father's calling, was Grimwade's shepherd and he had lived at the cottage all his life. He had never noticed the place, he just lived in it, but he knew that nothing had changed there for a century. Nothing, that is, except for the arrival of the tap.

Ted could just remember his mother carrying clanking galvanised buckets down to the well by the gate, winding the handle, bringing water up to the top and filling the buckets carefully. Then she laboured up the path again, a full bucket at the end of each elongated arm.

The old Mr Grimwade had laid a pipe from the farm and installed running water. It was a wonderful thing to have water on tap.

Ted knew very few people, but a great many sheep. His ears were tuned to their calls; the childish bleat of lambs, the guttural chuckle of elderly ewes, the sounds of contentment, the cries of distress. He knew the icy nights and dawns of lambing time, the heat and jostle and noise of dipping and everything in between. He knew of changes in the weather before they happened. And he was accompanied everywhere by his black and white sheepdog whose eager eyes never left his face.

There had been a succession of dogs over the years and they all looked alike. They bore the brief, unimaginative names that shepherds have always given their dogs; Tam, Bess, Kep, Nip, Jack, Nell and finally Jess.

Ted and Jess began to feel their age at about the same time but they kept on working, and at the end of the day's work they followed the routine of years. They walked slowly back to the cottage, where Ted poked the small range into life and put the kettle on. Then he fetched a battered enamel saucepan, lifted the lid and cut a large chunk off the boiled lights in it. With a clatter, he dropped the meat into a metal baking dish on the brick floor. Jess made short work of it, rattling the dish into a corner to get the last bits up. Ted filled her water bowl, made himself a large corned beef sandwich and a pot of tea, then he and Jess spent the evening sitting by the range.

Even without putting a light on, Ted could see Jess's dim outline at his feet and make out the white speck of fur above each of her eyes. Without looking, he could reach up to the cupboard beside him and bring out his pipe, matches and tobacco pouch. He enjoyed his smoke, resting the stem on his pipe tooth.

Eventually he would open the cottage door, sniff the air and listen to hear that all was well with the sheep, before shuffling to the outside privy while Jess dashed off in the shadows. As he turned back into the cottage, she would be waiting for him to go in and open the door to the stairs. She clattered ahead and leapt on to the iron bed among the scramble of ticking and blankets and old coats that served as bedding for both of them.

Ted removed his cap and his jacket and lay down. All day, every day, Ted wore the same clothes. On his head was a cap with a press stud at the front. On his feet were strong boots. On the rest of him was a collarless shirt, and a suit which had been bought by old Mr Grimwade in 1953 and then had outlived old Mr Grimwade by thirty-two years.

His son, Ted's present boss, had asked, 'Any good to you,

Ted? My dad thought a lot of you, so don't be offended will you?'

Ted was not offended because of the manner in which the gift was made. He put the suit on, and kept it on for the next thirty years. The good black suiting gradually faded until it was the colour of a dark December afternoon. When a button fell off, Ted opened the bradawl on his pocket knife and made a hole where it had been. He then tied a piece of string between it and the matching buttonhole.

This method of mending eventually ruled out undressing altogether, so he stopped bothering. In winter he wore fingerless gloves, and in summer he did not.

In the mornings. Ted would wake to find Jess looking at him intently from six inches away, her tail thumping gently. He would struggle up, in the dark as often as not, creak down the stairs and let her out. Then he would put the kettle on to boil, eat a couple of slices of bread and drop four slices into Jess's tin with a good helping of milk.

When she was ready to come in, Jess never hurled herself against the door or scratched at it, she just went 'sniff, sniff' at the bottom, in the gap where the winter wind cut in.

As Ted began to feel his age more and more, so did Jess. Her eyes became milky, and after she lost the use of her back legs quite suddenly, the farmer arrived with the Landrover.

'I'll take her down to the vet, Ted. Morris will look after her.'

They both knew what he meant.

They put her into the back of the Landrover on a piece of sacking and Mr Grimwade drove away. Ted sat by his fire and missed the dog fiercely.

'All over, Ted,' said the farmer when he returned. 'She was a good dog to you.'

Ted said nothing for a bit, then declared, 'Well, that's me

111

done for. What's the use of a shepherd without a dog? I can't train up a youngster at my age.'

He would have liked to select and train a pup again, but he was a realist. He was too old for shepherding but it was hard to admit, so he justified his retirement.

'She beat me to it, boss, but I think my working days are over too.'

The farmer put a hand on his shoulder. 'I tell you what, you can stay on on the cottage if you want — keep it warm like. I shall sell it off one day, but not while you need it. It wouldn't be right not to have a Gregory in the place. The old house wouldn't know itself.'

Ted nodded several times, which covered for all the words he wanted to say but couldn't.

'That's very kind of you boss — and thank you.'

The farmer understood.

With a new shepherd living in, up at the farmhouse, Ted's days were quiet. He sat all day in the sunken armchair by his grate and hardly moved. He enjoyed being warm all day instead of fighting the weather and increasing stiffness and tiredness. But he did miss Jess. Her presence had been like a shadow, anticipating his direction. She no longer warmed half his bed so he stopped using it. He just sat in the armchair day and night.

Once a week the mobile shop stopped outside and the driver came up to the cottage with Ted's order. Five tins of corned beef, five tins of sardines and three sliced loaves.

Ted hardly needed to move at all. However, one night, shuffling back from the outside privy, he fell and lay all night on the doorstep. The postman found him early in the morning and fetched the farmer. The farmer fetched the doctor who gave him a thorough going over.

'I'm going to put you down for a place at St Agnes.'

Ted rumbled, 'I don't want to go to no home.'

The doctor smiled cheerfully, picked up his bag and strode out.

For a few weeks, nothing happened. Sometimes young Mrs Grimwade looked in, bringing a piece of pie, a helping of treacle pudding or half a cake.

'Anything you want, Ted?' She would enquire and kindly fill his coal bucket without being asked. 'I'll pop in again,' she would say, and hurry out into the fresh air.

One day, Mr Grimwade said, 'Ted, I'm going to put the cottage on the market. You won't be pushed out until there's a place for you at St Agnes, but the agent will want to bring people round occasionally. That all right?'

Ted nodded.

The first dozen people who came with the agent recoiled as soon as they looked inside and backed out hastily saying, 'Not quite what we had in mind . . .' But one young couple came right in and actually looked round. They were called Dominic and Tricia Buckman and they talked in tactfully quiet voices.

'Just look at the state of the ceiling, and we'll have to to something about this . . . and this . . . but look at the dear little cupboard! And the stairs behind a door!'

The agent pointed out the original window catches, the wrought iron window hooks, the view across the valley, the good vegetable garden, the sound brick floors, the low lintels. At the end of an hour, the young woman approached Ted.

'We think we could be really happy here, Mr Gregory. We want to have a real country cottage for our very first home and we think this is just what we're looking for. When it's all . . . when we've done a few repairs, we hope you'll come and visit us. Now . . .' she added,' is there anything you need?'

Ted glanced at his empty coal bucket but didn't like to ask her to refill it, so they went away to talk business with the agent.

When the social worker came to fetch Ted and take him to the home, she asked. 'What about your things? Haven't you got any luggage? No belongings? No change of . . . No. Well. Is this your razor on the sink? I'll pop it in the car then. No pyjamas or flannel? All right Mr Gregory, let's get you out of your chair then.'

She helped him up and he wobbled bow-legged to the car. As she helped him in and put his piece of three-inch luggage into the glove compartment, he did not look back at the house at all. He sat expressionless as they made the short drive down the hill to the village and through the gates of St Agnes' Home for the Elderly.

The first thing that happened was a bath. A vigorous woman cut the bits of string that held his jacket on, stripped him and helped him into the water. He was washed and dried, new clothes were brought in and she helped him dress in underwear, a shirt with buttons, twill trousers, socks with no holes, bedroom slippers and a Fair Isle sleeveless jumper. His suit and cap had disappeared.

'Don't you look smart!' she approved. 'Now here's your razor and some new blades for it, and some soap and a brush. You have a nice shave and I'll be back in a minute.'

When she returned, she showed him to his own bedroom, 'With a cupboard for your clothes, and a nice chest of drawers, and a basin, and some pretty pictures. You can also have your own photos and knick-knacks if you want.'

Ted stared dumbly at her.

'Shall I leave you on your own for a bit?' she asked sympathetically.

Ted nodded.

She went out and Ted sat on a steel-framed chair, trying to come to terms with the Fair Isle sweater. He got up and shuffled round the room, looking at the pictures. There were swans on a lake, kittens in a basket and two old-fashioned lads in frocks holding a lamb. He peered at it.

When the woman returned he asked, 'What's that?' pointing.

'The picture? It says *Our Lord and St John,*' she read.

'I mean, what breed? It's not like anything I've ever seen. Terrible legs on it.'

She laughed and led him in to tea.

In between meals, Ted was too shy to sit in the day room among the other residents, most of whom were ladies with perms and glasses. He stayed in his bedroom and at mealtimes one of the assistants would tap at his door.

'Come on, Ted, there's a lovely meal waiting in the dining room!' And she would put her arm round his waist and take him down the passage calling, 'Here I come with my new boyfriend.'

Ted ate anything that was put in front of him; from porridge and sausages at breakfast, to stew and fruit and custard at dinner, ending up with a good tea of fish fingers and cake — with cups of tea and more cups of tea.

The helpers laughed good naturedly. 'The new boy-friend's got a good appetite.'

Ted, who had heard very little laughter in his life, began to enjoy himself.

He was taken to a barber, then to a chiropodist and for the first time for years, he was able to walk without pain in his feet. It was a miracle. He was always warm too and never hungry. And although he was not very sociable, he started sitting in the day room, to look about him and to stare uncomprehending at the television.

Once a week a lady came and played the piano. He found he knew the words of the songs Pack Up Your Troubles and Keep The Home Fires Burning. Everyone sang and Ted joined in silently.

Once a week, a lady came to do Keep Fit with them all.

'Fit?' thought Ted. 'I'd like to see her turn an ewe for shearing or carry a fat lamb uphill for a mile on her shoulders.'

But he stood in a ring with the others and punched the air, flexed his knees and circled his head. It passed the time.

Sometimes at night, Ted felt the weight of Jess on his bed and he put out a hand to touch her fur but there was none, and the weight melted as his consciousness returned.

Christmas arrived with streamers and paper bells and a Christmas tree that reminded Ted of a gorsebush after a gale, so full was it with foil and fluff and paper things. Some Brownies came with Brown Owl and stood to attention to sing Little Jesus Sweetly Sleep, then rushed back to their meeting in-the hall down the road.

Ted received three cards; one with a Nativity scene from Matron, one with a stage coach from the Grimwades, and one with two daft rabbits hugging under mistletoe from Dominic and Tricia. He read, *'You must come and visit us soon.'*

Ted put the cards back in their envelopes but an assistant said, 'No, no — you stand them on your chest of drawers — like this. Now it looks like Christmas.'

Everyone had a little present from Matron on Christmas Day and the dinner was like nothing Ted had ever eaten. He enjoyed himself without reminiscing or comparing. He gave no thought to the years of working out in the dark fields with just a countryman's feeling that Christmas was special because of its link with animals and byres. His only present then had been a small, gently curved bottle, bought first by old Mr Grimwade, then by his son. Thud on the table. 'There you are, Ted, that'll help keep the cold out. Merry Christmas to you.'

His reply was invariably, 'And to you and your good lady, boss.'

And that had been the end of the festivities.

Dominic and Tricia started work on the boring bits of the house first. A new roof, a damp course, wiring and plumbing. Then the lean-to scullery was pulled down and replaced by a new kitchen extension with bathroom above. The brick floor was pulled up, heating pipes put in, pine floorboards laid. They took out the original windows and replaced them with pretty diamond panes. They put a stable door at the kitchen end and built a roomy storm-porch across the front door to keep the draught out. They went to the Furnu-Home Warehouse and bought two beams made of plastic that could easily be mistaken for oak, to fix below the living room ceiling.

'Now it's really feeling like a country cottage,' said Tricia delighted.

Next, they chose Victorian style kitchen units and pine dining table and chairs. They pulled out Ted's old range and put in an electric fire with glowing log effect and a copper canopy. As a finishing touch they added brass fire irons, quite clean and new and likely to stay that way.

Then, as a surprise for Tricia, Dominic had the cupboard by the fire taken out and replaced with a white alcove for her foreign doll collection. And after much searching, they found a spiral staircase to take the place of the steep, narrow flight behind the latched door.

They hugged each other with joy.

'And in the spring,' promised Dominic, 'we'll have the garden laid out. Sunken — to utilise the slope, with a pool and a willow and a wishing well.'

For Christmas he gave Tricia a real old butterchurn to stand in the corner with flowers on. With much giggling and secrecy, Tricia had a genuine cartwheel delivered for his present — to lean against the outside of the house.

Dominic had an inspired idea. 'Let's have a board made with *The Old Wheelwright's Cottage* on it,' he suggested.

'That's a bit long,' said Tricia, 'why not just *Wheelwright's?*'

She was delighted with his pleasure in her present, and the board was ordered and put up on the gatepost.

'We really must ask our old man to come up and visit us,' they said to one another over the next few months. 'One day we really will — and won't he be surprised at the change?'

Meanwhile, they enjoyed every moment of living in their cottage. They gave little dinners for friends, and while Tricia popped cherries on each melon slice, Dominic showed the exclaiming guests round their *find*, proudly opening every cupboard, and switching everything on and off for their entertainment. Then they sat down to ratatouille from the microwave and luscious desserts from the freezer shop. If anyone had shown Tricia a skinned rabbit and some onions and bayleaves, she would probably have passed out.

One day at the office, Dominic muttered, 'I'd better give Trish a ring, she wasn't feeling too well this morning when I left.'

'Oh?' enquired a colleague.

'No, she didn't even want the cup of tea I took up to her.'

His friend smiled.

'She hasn't gone off coffee too by any chance?' he asked.

Dominic was surprised. 'Funny you should say that . . .'

There was laughter.

'Congratulations, Daddy,' they said. 'She'll be wanting green apples and kippers next.'

And their long-distance diagnosis was correct.

Proudly, Dominic indulged her every whim. Being a sensible girl of course, she did not crave apples and kippers at all — but she did want pickled onions at the oddest times.

Dominic supposed that it was just another of her fancies when she began to demand daily that it was time they fulfilled their Christmas promise of an invitation to Ted. It was September already and still they had not asked him round to see the place. Obligingly, Dominic rang the matron and said he would fetch Mr Gregory on Sunday afternoon.

To welcome him, Tricia stood beaming in the new doorway. She hardly recognised the clean, white-haired old gentleman who stepped from the car.

He looked about him for a minute, getting his bearings. He glanced up at the farmhouse across the field, his eyes and ears seeking sheep on the hill above. Then he walked in.

Dominic smiled. 'Not bad, eh, Mr Gregory?' and proceeded to offer the guided tour: opening and shutting things, switching lights on and off.

` Ted just looked about him as if he was in a completely strange house and politely said, 'Grand,' every now and again.

His eye lit upon white knitting on a low stool. Tricia saw his glance.

'Yes, we're having a baby — isn't it exciting? Next April.' The old shepherd nodded. 'Grand. April. A good month. All the summer to grow strong.'

He looked at the new kitchen, ignored the Victorian units but questioned the strings of plastic onions, garlic and peppers which hung on the wall.

'Oh,' laughed Tricia, 'they're just to look nice. The real peppers and onions are in the deep freeze and I use garlic out of the tube.'

Ted's face registered nothing. He turned to the spiral staircase, and Dominic started up it, to lead him to see the pink bathroom with shower and bidet, and the brass bed with patchwork duvet cover and matching curtains.

Ted shook his head.

'No, no. I'll stay on the ground if you don't mind,' he said, 'and you'll need to watch your little one on them stairs.'

For some reason, Tricia was annoyed. She changed the subject by offering a cup of tea. Ted's eye went to where the grate and kettle should have been.

'If its all the same to you, I'll be setting out,' he said, 'I reckon the walk back will do me good.'

'Let me run you back in the car — it's no trouble,' offered Dominic.

Ted shook his head. 'Much obliged to you, but I'd like the walk. It's a grand evening.'

They escorted him down to the gate and he gazed open-mouthed at his transformed cabbage-patch. He pointed to the corner by the gate.

'What's that?'

'It's a wishing well,' they answered happily.

'Is it now? Is it now?' And he made the first joke he had ever made in his life. 'I wish you well,' he said, and tried to laugh but it came out as an old man's cough.

He turned and set off down the hill. Dominic and Tricia lingered by the gate in case he waved, but he didn't.

'Do you think he liked it?' Tricia asked.

'Of course he did. He was probably even a bit envious.'

As they came in again, something clattered in the kitchen, sounding like a metal dish on the floor.

'What was that?' asked Tricia.

'Something must have slipped in the cupboard. Don't worry about it,' reassured Dominic.

They looked about briefly, but nothing had moved that they could see. Tricia made a meal in the microwave, and then they sat down with clear consciences to watch television.

It was just a month later that the telephone rang. It was the matron from St Agnes to say that Ted had passed away suddenly. He had had a massive heart attack in the night and died without pain. The funeral was to take place on Thursday at two o'clock.

Dominic and Tricia were really very sorry. They were young enough for death to be quite a novelty but the novelty value did not extend to their attending the funeral. They thought it might be bad for the baby. Anyway, Mr and Mrs Grimwade were sure to go.

'Do you think he's watching us?' wondered Tricia, sensitive in her condition.

'Don't be silly!' scoffed Dominic, 'I'm not having you upset. Here have a look at the new Mothercare catalogue.'

Tricia flicked through the pages of pinafore dresses. Her symptoms, her changing weight and shape were of constant interest to them both. It was a joke that when sitting down, she could balance a cup of tea on the developing ledge in front of her.

'Mind Maradona doesn't kick it into goal,' laughed Dominic and thereafter, whenever he came in from work he would ask, 'How's Maradona?'

'Kicking nicely, thank you sir,' Tricia would answer. One day she said, 'If it's a boy I'd like to call him Edward, after our old man.'

'And if it's a girl, Donna after Maradona,' joked Dominic.

Another Christmas passed and spring came with the far away cries of sheep and lambs on the hill beyond the farm.

'I'm beginning to wonder,' panted Tricia as she started her fifth trip up staircase that evening, 'if this is the best staircase we could have chosen. Or perhaps I'd settle for a downstairs loo.'

After a short time, she yelled from upstairs, 'Dominic — get the car, get my case, I've started!' and she hurried down, her face alight with excitement and apprehension.

Dominic sat her in a chair. 'Now don't dash about, I'll get everything.'

He sprinted up the stairs, grabbed the suitcase and rushed back down, feet hardly touching the treads.

'Don't move!' he said, hurrying out to get the car. The cottage door swung gently and there was silence.

From beneath the door Tricia heard, 'Sniff, sniff.' She was puzzled. Then she heard it again. 'Sniff, sniff.'

The car started up and Dominic came back in to help her.

'Dominic, I heard something!' she fretted. 'Something sniffed under the door.'

'Nonsense!' Dominic was anxious, impatient. 'Come on, love, let's get you in the car.'

'But I did!'

He hustled her out and helped her carefully into the passenger seat.

'One of your fancies, I expect,' he soothed.

Little Edward was born that night and his arrival was the apex of the country cottage idyll. After a short time, Dominic and Tricia began to wish they had a little more room and considered building on again. But it was young Edward who brought matters to a head the day he bounced and ricocheted down the spiral staircase. He cut his cheek, bumped his head and yelled the place down. That was when his parents decided that, fun though the cottage had been, it was time to move to a family house, preferably in Georgian style.

They put the cottage on the market.

'Made a few changes here, haven't you?' observed the agent. 'Very nice. Very nice.' He made eager notes in his book.

With pride, Tricia said, 'It's got a ghost too.'

The agent, visualising headless horsemen and ghostly bodies swinging from gibbets, mentally added another thousand to the price.

Until they moved out, Dominic and Tricia quite often heard the clatter of the metal dish on a stone floor, the squeak of a cupboard, the click of a door latch which had long since gone to the council tip. And once, down by the gate not far from the wishing well, the unmistakable sound of a galvanised bucket.

Against The Grain

Richard Newman

You know, I cringe when I see the shoddy way they make modern furniture. Things aren't like they used to be!

When I started as an apprentice cabinet-maker, everything was made out of solid timber: walnut, oak or mahogany. Stuff then was built to last. Times have certainly changed! These days, they ruddy well throw things together and you're lucky if you get a couple of years' use out of them. Even in the funeral business, ninety-nine per cent of the caskets are now made out of blockboard with a bit of veneer stuck on.

Well, they won't put me in one of those things; in fact, I've already built my own. Solid oak it is and lined with some pure silk that I picked up from the Northern Shroud and Coffin Lining Company over in Bradford. Luckily, they were having a closing-down sale so I got it for next to nowt.

I'm going to be embalmed when I go. I mean, you never know, they might find out how to bring people back to life in a few years time so I might as well look my best — just in case. If not, my body should last nearly as long as the casket, with it being oak. It's beautiful wood.

I've got stacks of timber lying around the house, accumulated over the years I spent working at Herbert Sykes's. I just couldn't bear to put it into the pot-bellied stove so I sneaked it into the back of my van when old Sykesy wasn't looking. It's a damn good job my wife isn't still alive; though it'd be bloody awful for her if she was — she's been buried nine month. She'd've gone mad with so much wood in the house. I've just brought in five tons from the garden shed.

I can still see her face now when I walked in from work with a bundle of scrap timber.

'Ron!' she screamed, 'We're not having any more of that rubbish in here!'

I didn't use to argue with her. No, what I said was, 'Fair enough then, love. I'll find a corner in the shed for it.'

Then what I'd do was wait until she'd gone shopping or something, and get it into the house sharpish. The shed was full to bursting even in those days. Not that she'd notice of course; she spent most of her life in front of the flamin' television set. Eventually though, I did manage to get her away from the telly for good.

Incredibly, I got her interested in wood — in a very roundabout sort of way, you understand. You see, she smoked very heavily did Doris, a hundred and twenty a day. A proper chainy she was, forever lighting up. Well, as you can imagine, the ashtrays were full of tab ends and matches.

So one day I said to her — with the thought of all that wasted match-wood in mind, 'Lovey, why don't you have a go at building something out of all those dead matches?'

'Not ruddy likely,' she said. 'We've enough with one nutter in the house buggering about with bits of fire-wood.'

'No, lovey,' I said soothingly. 'You misunderstand. Take a look at these.'

I pushed a book under her nose that I'd got out of the library — Matchstick Creations From All Over The World. And it told you how to go about building your own.

'Surely you could do better than these?' I coaxed.

I knew she could never resist a challenge and within a week, she was hit by matchstick fever. Our television set had never been unplugged for so long; not since 1965 when we couldn't afford to pay the license.

Well, she got totally carried away with the job. She built all sorts of weird creations. Not the usual boring stuff either, such as Tower Bridge or Spanish galleons. No, her stuff was very individual. In fact, after a while, she got to be a ruddy nuisance, especially when she started to use me as her model.

'Hold it right there a minute, will you,' she shouted one afternoon when I'd just settled on the outside loo. I had to sit there flamin' hours while she copied my position on the lavvy. I had a red ring on my arse for three days afterwards.

You might find this hard to believe but let me tell you, when she'd finished with those matchsticks it was a ruddy masterpiece. She's managed to get the detail absolutely spot-on; right down to the strained look on my face and the trousers crumpled round my ankles.

She could have gone far could Doris, with the right education. Very artistic she was, with an uncanny eye for detail. It's a shame she didn't start in the sixties, her work would have sold for a bomb. They went for anything weird and wonderful in them days.

She could be a pain at time, though, with her still-life studies. For instance, she'd made my favourite meal, spaghetti bolognese. I should have realised why!

'Don't move, Ron. That's fantastic,' she suddenly shrieked.

For the next umpteen hours I had to sit perfectly still with my mouth crammed full of spaghetti. The times I've wished I'd left her to her television programmes! Anyway, like the others, when it was finished it really did look superb. The facial contortion was to a tee and the model so accurate, there were strands of spaghetti curling up from the plate and into my pursed-lipped mouth. Mind you, I went right off spaghetti bolognese after that session.

Another — On Reflection — she called it, was a side view of herself naked in the bath. And I had to hold the flamin' mirror. It took hours to finish 'cos the steam affected the glue.

A major piece that she did over Christmas '74 — a personal favourite of mine — was her interpretation of the night sky. First she covered all the corners in our bedroom ceiling with sheets of cardboard to create a domed effect. Then she painted the walls and ceiling a deep blue-black shade. Finally she meticulously applied her incredible matchstick solar system, dabbing the match-heads with luminous paint. It was a mammoth task. We even had to knock through into the spare room to accommodate some distant galaxy or other.

Admittedly it didn't look much in the daylight, but come darkness, it was out of this world! You could even make out the craters on the moon's surface. It actually made the London Planetarium look like kid's stuff. Sometimes, I'd lie awake at night and look up at the stars.

It was mind boggling to think that the snoring body next to me in curlers and hair-net had created such a stagger-ing work of art!

One of her last works, a bit morbid, mind, and she filled the ruddy attic with it, was a perfect scale model of the Necropolis Cemetery. There were crosses and tombs, chapels and obelisks, all in their exact positions. If you looked at it from the side she'd done a sort of cross-sectional effect so you could see into some of the graves, complete with miniature coffins and skeletons.

Apparently, her grandmother was buried in the Necrop-olis Cemetery, which is a fair distance away, so that's why Doris decided to do a copy of it — so she could put flowers on it whenever she liked.

Funny though. After she'd finished the cemetery project she became obsessed with her own death. She built herself a coffin out of matchsticks.

'They can take me off in that when the time comes,' she sighed.

'Don't be ridiculous, woman,' I exploded. 'There's years left in you yet! Anyway, we're not having you leaving this house feet-first in a contraption like that. I'd be the laughing stock of the street, me being a master craftsman and in the trade. If and when you do go, it'll be in style. A best oak job like mine.'

Somehow though, she never seemed to be the same after finishing the coffin. She seemed to lose all interest in everything.

One of the reasons she stopped her matchstick building was because her sister Elsie bought her a fancy cigarette lighter for her birthday. Once the old matches had run out, that was it, no more life studies, nothing.

She was, however, smoking more and more, and within two months of giving up her hobby she was gone.

The funeral was an embarrassment! I know everybody was laughing behind my back, but in the end I let them use her flamin' matchstick casket because of her stupid sister.

'That's what she really wanted and that's what she'll have,' she insisted.

Then, after she'd gone, Lord knows why, but I suddenly got the building-bug myself. Not old matchsticks though, not bloody likely! I used quality stuff and put my old skills to good use. You see, one evening I was reading this encyclopaedia when this plan of Noah's Ark caught my eye.

I studied the dimensions carefully, and realised that I'd more than enough wood round the house to have a go at building one of my own.

That was almost a year ago. It's been a bigger job than I'd thought. Give it another ten to twelve months and I'll be able to try it out on the canal.

Changes

Una Stothard Smith

My father was my friend. More than that, he was my security. We were lucky. We lived in a railway house that went with his job and we had a privilege ticket to the end of the British Isles once a year.

My mother told this proudly to neighbours who never went further than a day trip to Belle View for a holiday.

'Your father is a good provider,' she told us. We were three children and we knew that already.

At our house we had a black-leaded iron grate with two ovens and hot water always at the ready. We also had a big deal table with stockinged mahogany legs that stood in the centre of the room.

Above the bread oven was a warming oven with a drop down door. My father used to drop this door, draw up his wheel-back chair and sit, ankles crossed, with his feet on the shelf it created. To make it all comfortable, he balanced on the back legs of his chair and rocked.

It was a regular thing, half an hour before my bed time, for me to climb like a Chinese acrobat from the front legs of the chair and without a by-your-leave find myself a seat in the angle of his lap. He didn't nurse me so much as pemit me to be there.

I occupied myself sewing cross stiches into buckram canvas with brightly coloured wool, threaded beads or recited 'in, over, through, off' to the scarf I was knitting for my Sunny Jim, an Uncle Sam replica that came with the Force Cornflakes coupons.

Sometimes my father closed his eyes to listen to his Grieg records which he played on our phonograph, and sometimes he read his Science magazine.

It wasn't so much that he played with me or made a fuss of me, it was more that we did what we wanted to do separately — but together. It was the most beautiful relationship I have ever known.

He was extremely proud of what he called my 'sensitivity'. He entered me for the Mrs Sunderland verse speaking competition, a nationwide contest held annually in our town. Every day he put me through my paces. I loved it. I adored his undivided attention.

'We'll do it once if we do it well, once if it's poor and twice if it's so-so.'

It was mostly so-so, which meant it had to be recited again. I didn't mind. In fact, it didn't matter how many times I had to say it so long as it was for him.

There were times, mostly at weekends, when he told me to 'Fetch your bonnet, we'll have a walk over to your An Temla's.' My An Temla was his sister and she called him, 'Yar Jack.' My mother said she was 'Your daddy's side,' but I liked her anyway.

Often he'd tell me to 'get your shooting boots on, I'm going to the garage.' My legs were like matchsticks and I took three runs to his every stride. I was his shadow wherever he went.

I remember picking up bright stones on the way and running to show them to him, but I can't remember playing games. Games were not for us.

At the garage, all I ever seemed to do was mess about with his vice and dig in the dirt with a stick. All this doesn't sound very exciting but the sun seemed always to be shining. It wasn't what we did — it was what we were. We were friends and we were close. When we were together, we were content simply to be.

I can't remember him ever cuddling or making a fuss of me. But I remember the feel of the towel as he threaded it between my toes to free them of sand. And I remember my sou'wester half covering my eyes when he secured it with his scarf one day when it poured down as we walked home from my An Temla's.

Once, at Flamborough Head, we walked on the cliff tops together and the force of the gale lifted me clean off my feet. I had no fear though. He held me quite firmly. I knew I was safe.

I remember the day he came home from work in the heavy snow. He'd been out all night keeping the line clear so that trains could run on time. He was wearing his army greatcoat for extra warmth and the puttees he'd worn in the trenches. He huddled up to the fire still wearing them and wouldn't eat any dinner.

I was upset when he went back to work without dinner and I didn't know why. Then next day, I was sent to my Grandma's. My daddy had gone back to bed.

My friend saw me getting on the bus. She asked 'How's your daddy?'

I stood on the bus step and a large tear came. The conductor said, 'Hold tight,' — and I think I knew I wasn't going to see him again.

The seriousness of his pneumonia was kept from me. I had to sleep in my Grandma's big bed because she had gone to sleep in mine. That was the only explanation I was given.

I spent the time in the charge of my Aunt Clara. She wasn't really my aunt, she was my uncle's wife. She was rough with me and showed me how to catch a chicken and wring its neck. She held it by its feet and its head wobbled, its coxcomb bright and its wing feathers shining like a spill of petrol. In play she swung it towards me and laughed because I ran.

In my Grandma's bed I dreamed of hobgoblins who chased me. To escape I tried to climb over a wall. There was a sheer drop on the other side. I couldn't go forward and I couldn't get back. The goblin gained and I jumped. Falling, falling; waking in my Grandma's big wide bed.

Eyes open to the black, I waited in dark fear until I became accustomed to the shadows and I could see stars, comforting shafts of God, through the stone mullions.

After ten days, a message came on Mrs Crowther's telephone. Their chauffeur came to deliver it. He whispered the message to my Aunt Clara.

'You've to catch the next bus,' my Aunt Clara said. 'They want to see you at school.'

I sensed she was lying. I thought it was the kiddy catcher who was after me. I was afraid of the kiddy catcher but it was a relief to get away from my Aunt Clara. She used to put me in the cellar if I was naughty. She said Mickey was down there picking his toe nails and Mickey, whoever he was, terrified me. I was glad I'd been sent for. I caught the next bus. I ran in home first. 'I'm going up to see my daddy,' I said. Three women sat there. My mother, my Grandmother and my An Tannie. Just sitting there they were — not eating or doing needlework or cleaning spoons. Just sitting there. I wondered why nobody was upstairs looking after my daddy. It was strange. Grown-ups were hard to understand.

My mother said, 'There's not time to go up now, love, you'll be late for school.' Gullible, I did what Mother told me because I always did. There was a greyness about her. She looked cold.

But even when I came home from school, she insisted I ate my dinner before she let me go upstairs. I cleaned my plate because I knew I had to.

Then my An Tannie said, 'We'll take you to *see* him now.' It was the way she said *see*.

I walked between them, three of us in line. My Grandma in front and my An Tannie behind me.

We reached the landing. The bedroom door was open. I saw my daddy's bed, white and starched and still. I cowered back and slid down the landing wall until I was sitting on my heels.

'Don't be a silly girl,' my An Tannie said. 'Don't you want to see your daddy?'

She took hold of my wrist in a vice-like grip and pulled me to my feet. I didn't resist.

Obediently, I waited by the starched bed for them to lift the monogrammed handkerchief and then I went back downstairs and stood by the big deal table.

My hands and face were washed and I was taken to be measured for a new coat.

'Navy blue is right for little ones,' my Grandma said.

'She can wear her black patent dancing shoes,' my mother said. 'They've not been had on since the pantomime.'

To my father's delight, I had danced a solo in the children's pantomime at Christmas and now it was February.

'Children soon get over it. They don't feel things the same,' my An Tannie said.

They were telling me these things — but not telling me. Saying them to each other, they were giving me my instructions.

There wasn't enough room in our small living room for all the people who came. His oak coffin was under the window and the curtains were drawn. The room was heavy with flowers and the sweet smell of him.

My father was young, it was considered a tragedy. People spilled onto the pavement outside our front door. I was taken out there too, to look at the horses, by the man with ribbons down the back of his high silk hat.

When I got outside, neighbours were gathered down the street to pay their respects and watch the cortege leave. They had quiet, grave faces.

'That's his little girl,' they whispered.

The wind blew. It ruffled black feather flowers in silver vases on top of the horses' harness and it jingled little silver discs fixed in silver brackets on the bridle.

I shivered in a cold kind of excitement. Similar to the

excitement I had felt at the pantomime, when I knew everybody was watching me dance.

'There's the little one,' the neighbours said. And I felt they wanted me to do something.

I didn't know what was expected of me. I was wearing the black patent shoes I had worn in the pantomime, so I did the little dance. I did it very nicely — the very best I could. My daddy had been so proud at Christmas when everybody clapped. You couldn't have wiped the smile off his face. But nobody clapped today.

Then they came out of the house and all the men removed their hats. My Grandma swung the carriage low as she got in and the men helped her. I sat in the corner under her big taffeta dress. She almost crushed me.

Nobody took any notice of me.

When I got down from the carriage, it was my An Temla who took my hand and paddled me to the grave. She hadn't been in our carriage. She was my daddy's side, you see.

The house was empty when we got back. Somebody had tidied up and lit a fire. My mother took off her new black hat and smoothed the taffeta ribbon. She placed in on the table and stirred the fire.

'I'll make a drink of tea,' she said.

There was a lonely hole in my chest but I didn't tell anybody about it. My mother had enough worries without me bothering her. We were living in a railway house; a house that went with my father's job.

On the table, next to my mother's hat was a parcel. It had arrived when we were out. The printing on top said — London & Scottish Railways. Head Office: Aire Street, Leeds.

My mother opened it. It was a black morocco presentation bible in recognition of my father's services. There was also a letter — signed by the chairman. My mother read it aloud.

It said, 'Since the property you occupy is intended for the use of railway employees, it is regretted, that in the circumstances, it is necessary to ask you to vacate the premises forthwith.'

It didn't say anything about when my daddy would be coming back for his clothes.

I went into the yard to wait and to play in the dirt with a stick.

Reunion

Bill Lang

I was humming that old tune in my head 'This heart of mine is doing very well . . .' and thinking of all the times we'd played that record back in '46. Slowly I drove past the ruin of the five-hundred-bed hostel; now an electric cable store with a battered Nissen hut still in the far corner. Then I pressed on till I found a lay-by near Four Lane Ends where I switched off the engine and looked over the valley to get my bearings.

There were too many changes. Where were the winding wheels and framework of the pit? Gone — and in its place, convenient for the M62, a jumble of lorry parks and big firms. One of them a skin products manufacturer I remembered from '44. Pit lads used to get Vaseline from there to get the coal dust out of their eyelids.

Forty years away is a long time, and even now I couldn't think why I'd had this sudden urge to drive over here.

Not many houses left, but the Pit Manager's house was still there. Big place, dark grey stone, with lots of rooms to emphasise the difference. The master in his mansion, the mastered in their hutches.

But Fred had been both. Born in a humble cottage, he started down the pit during the first war and worked his way through the grades up to manager by the time of the '26 strike.

I smiled, recollecting a one-day strike when he was boss. It happened to be pay day and the strikers queued at the window for their wages. But Fred had secreted the clerks in the back of the office and told the strikers the office staff had come out in solidarity. So there was no pay that day and that soon broke the strike.

Would Fred still be there in his mansion? In his eighties now, maybe widowed and alone? Or would British Coal have sold it off to be turned into flats?

There was a long pause after I rapped the knocker but I was prepared to wait. I'd been up to the big house often enough and I knew those hallways and passages took some getting through.

Funny how Fred had taken a fancy to me, encouraging me to take the mining exams like he'd done — to become deputy at least. But I'd other ideas and I'd commitments back at the coast — Auntie, who'd brought me up.

Following the sound of light footsteps, the door was opened by a dark haired woman in her late fifties, her hair starting to streak white.

'Ivy,' I said, taken aback. 'What are you doing here?'

'It's Jim, isn't it? By lad, I never thought to see you back here. Must be forty years or more since you pushed off.'

'But we had some good times, Ivy,' I reminded her. 'Is Fred Green still here? Or have you got the house now? . . . Are you married, Ivy?'

'No, I was never wed. I had me eye on you,' she said mischievously, but with a note of candour in her voice. 'So when Fred lost his missus, he asked me to come as housekeeper. It's a lot of work though, and he's failing now — heart. Come in, he'll be pleased to see you, he still talks about you a lot.'

She took me through the passages to a big room at the back. Surprisingly, it still overlooked some green fields. The changes and the clutter were all at the front.

Fred got up slowly as we went in. 'Who the devil? Thee . . . And tha never came back did tha — till now?'

'You know how it is, Fred,' I muttered, ashamed that I hadn't made the effort before. 'Going back spoils the memories — it's never the same. And Auntie used to keep on at me. 'Don't go back. Don't marry a miner's daughter or you'll be sucked down.'

Fred's face reddened. 'Tha could have done a damned sight worse and tha knows it. And this Auntie? I seem to remember, ten bob a week off your pay slip went to her. Didn't leave thee much, did she?'

'But you and your missus were real good to me. You made up for it with the meals you gave me.'

'And tha went out with Ivy plenty didn't tha? But then she always stood her corner.'

Fred took a little white box out of his pocket and popped some particles in his mouth.

'It's grand to see thee. But can't say it helps my angina.' Then he leaned forward confidentially. 'Ivy had a bairn, you know. Grown up now and doing well in computers down London way. This bairn — I suppose tha'll say it were nowt to do with thee.'

'No,' I protested, 'Anyway, I don't believe it. Ivy was Chapel, real solid Chapel.'

He pointed the stem of his pipe into my chest. 'She set her cap at thee but tha were always set on getting away, so maybe it was love on the rebound. Chapel can't control all feelings.'

'We were all chapel in them days,' I said. 'You, me, Ivy and Auntie. Yes, Auntie was very much chapel-near-the-sea.'

'Tha could have made it to Manager if tha'd stayed — and I'll bet tha didn't do as well where tha went.'

It was true. A few seasonal joys, some bad employers intent on sweating the last drop out for the least wage. It wasn't until I got on a newspaper that I began to earn some real money. I'd considered going back after my divorce from Pauline, but by then I was too old for coal mining.

Fred told Ivy to make us a right high tea, bring out the silver teapot, and said she was to sit at the head of the table. Meanwhile, he puffed at his pipe and asked questions.

'Of course, when I got thee it was with the idea of thee staying put — for life.'

'You got me?' I interrupted fiercely. 'No way. I was called up, went down to the Labour Exchange and they sent me to Salthouse Colliery for a limited period. It was only intended to be three and a half years!'

'Tha can think that if tha wants!' Fred grinned. 'But I got thee and there's no two ways about it!

'How do you mean?'

'Well, I was always keen on football as a lad — player and watcher. I saw in t'Yorkshire Post, tha'd been picked for a trial with Scarborough so I kept an eye on thee form. Reporter said it would only be for a few months — before tha were called up. So I rang Scarborough Labour Exchange and arranged that when tha were called in tha'd be offered a job at Salthouse Colliery and nowt else. It worked. That's how come we had a full football team down pit. Think of it. Lads of your age were going up into t'front line first night in North Holland, they weren't coming back. Yours were a snug job working that donkey engine on nights. Right?'

'Right. But I never realised it was an arranged job. I wonder what Auntie would have said if she'd known?'

'Tha seems to think a lot of this Auntie. She must have been good to thee.'

'She was — but fierce Methodist. Kept me on the right line about Ivy . . . and about everything else.'

'That's as maybe.'

'Annie Crosby was her name. She lived just off Columbus Ravine.'

I fancied Fred stirred uneasily in his chair and reached for some more pills.

'I know that district well,' he said. 'Been plenty of times to conferences in the Spa, even been chairman. But my first trip there was a chapel outing and I was going with a lass I was fond of. We managed to get away from the others and take a stroll over Scalby Mills. There's a lot of rocks there. It was September time and all the regular visitors had gone so we had the place to ourselves.'

The memory brought a smile to his face. 'And as they say, one thing followed another. Chapel advises but sap rises — that's why I wouldn't have been very surprised if you and Ivy . . .' He left the suggestion unsaid.

'The lass I was with had a relative off North Side — she was called Crosby, but it's a common enough name — and we went there for tea instead of taking it with the rest of the gang. They gave us some looks though, going back on the charabanc. 'Where had we been?' they wanted to know. But they didn't know the half of it!'

He laughed and put a hand on his chest again. Then he leant forward, 'I've nobody now, though, have I? So I thought I might leave this place to Ivy — and you — when I go.'

Fred had bought the house from the Coal Board and I was overwhelmed by his offer — but it was far too big and I told him so.

'Well, sell it for offices. There's plenty of new businesses setting up round here. Get yourself a nice little bungalow over Airedale way.'

'Why me, Fred? What have I done to deserve that? I already owe you for saving my life by getting me into the pit during the war.'

There was a long, long pause. He clutched his chest as a spasm of pain circulated through.

'I'm going to tell thee why. I knew Auntie.'

He laughed at my look of surprise.

'I knew her all right because I was paying her as well as you. There'd have been too much scandal around here, so she took you in.'

He made no sense. My slow-wittedness agitated him.

'Don't you understand? he barked. 'You're my son.'

Another spasm seized him and he sagged back in his chair, rousing me from my shock. I jumped up and raced down the passage to the kitchen. 'Ivy!' I yelled. 'Ivy!'

Freedom

Lilian Whitely

My body twitched uncontrollably as I tried to communicate with my mother. My head rolled about in circles and my mouth yawned open in an effort to speak. Not one coherent word came out. I could only produce high-pitched noises which made no sense to anybody except me. I knew what I wanted to say but the sounds echoing round the room mocked my efforts. It was so frustrating I thought I would go mad.

I willed the strong-faced woman to turn and look at me so I could use my eyes to transmit messages. My mother understood me better than anyone, but now she was like a stranger, not the mother I loved and depended upon. I screamed louder but she continued to ignore my appeals as she stared into the glow of the fire.

The deep lines on her face reflected the strain of thirty-eight years of coping with a severely handicapped daughter. I needed to tell my mother that I understood the problems she now faced; the daunting prospect of now having to cope alone — without the help of my father.

Just a few hours earlier, he had been buried in the small cemetery, leaving behind two lonely, despondent women. If I could only get out of my chair and offer comfort. Then my body suddenly ceased its activity and I lay back limp; filled with the fear of my own helplessness and what the future held for me.

My birth, which should have brought joy, had destroyed my parents' marriage in a physical sense. While they retained a deep abiding affection for each other, which had seemed to grow stronger through the years, the sexual side of their love ended with my birth.

Before they realised I could understand, I'd overheard my parents discussing the subject of more children. Father insisted it was too great a risk, they could never cope with two handicapped children. I was to be an only child and to ensure it, their marriage became celibate. Once they realised that I understood their conversations, they ceased to discuss their marital relationship and the three of us settled into a style of living which remained unchanged until Father's death from a heart attack a few days ago.

I looked towards Mother again. She was still; her hands folded loosely on her lap. I was afraid and tried to speak again but couldn't. Then, with an almighty effort, I managed to produce the sound which meant Mother. She turned slowly, as though awakening, then with a deep sigh she raised herself slowly from her chair, came across the room and crouched in front of me till we were eye to eye.

She studied me for what seemed an age, then, in a very matter-of-fact voice, announced, 'Well, Sarah, you're going to be introduced to the outside world at last.'

Mother's words gradually struck home.

It was a dream come true. But what a pity Father had to die to release me from this loving prison. Many times I'd overheard Mother pleading to let me out into the world beyond the high walled backyard. He had been steadfast in his refusal; insistent on protecting me from the stares and ridicule which I might be subjected to. I was well cared for and loved, but I was so over-protected I rarely saw another human being besides my parents.

Today, for the first time ever, I had been left in the care of another person. The vicar's wife, a trained nurse, stayed with me while the funeral took place. What a joy it was to see a fresh face and hear a new voice. Mrs Wright didn't appear to notice that the conversation was one-sided and seemed totally at ease with me. She talked about adult things as though I was an equal, and explained the funeral procedure to me.

When she suggested I accompany Mother on a weekly visit to the cemetery to take flowers for Father's grave, I could hardly believe it. The prospect of it helped me in my grief.

He was a wonderful man in spite of keeping me hidden away. He read to me every evening and it was the highlight of my day. I was so familiar with the classics by the time I reached my teens, I could spend hours in day-dreams, reliving the lives of my favourite characters.

I would have liked to tell him what a joy his readings were; how increasingly important books became as I drifted into middle-age. The fantasy world he created was the only other world I knew. He knew my favourite stories but would tease me by pretending not to understand my signals when choosing.

Mother's voice eventually penetrated my excitement. 'Calm down, Sarah, calm down. If you make yourself ill, you won't be able to go out after all.'

Her soothing, crooning voice brought me out of the state I'd worked myself into. I tried to still the spasms and relax my body. There were times when I was sure I had some control over my body, but this wasn't apparent to Mother, who thought it was her calming influence which stilled the tremors.

Mother described to me my first journey into the unknown as she fed me strained food. I was almost too excited to eat.

Mrs Wright arrived soon after I'd been fed. She was such a kind person with a quiet but firm voice. Mother greeted her with a grateful smile.

'It's so good of you to help me, in fact the answer to my prayers. I didn't know how I was going to cope with bath and bed time. Sarah doesn't weigh very much but her disability makes her difficult to handle, especially now my back's giving me problems.'

'Only too glad to be of help, Mrs Jordan. I would have

offered before, but my husband said your husband wouldn't have any outside help.'

Bath time was another new experience. Mrs Wright's nursing skills soon became evident and I listened in admiration as she instructed Mother on how to lift me without hurting her back.

Mother had long ago become expert in coping with my double incontinence and later, my periods. That event had come as a shock the first time I saw Mother wrapping up the blood-stained cotton wool pad. I thought I must have some new, dreadful disease. Neither could I understand why Father left the room at these times — when he always helped to bath and dress me. I was left puzzled by this phenomenon and Mother never explained.

When daylight came at last, I was bursting with excitement. Already exhausted from the effort of washing and dressing me, which took well over an hour, Mother was flustered and breathless as she dusted the wheelchair and made it ready. These things had been so much easier with two pairs of hands.

The hardest task was in getting my body into the wheelchair. The least excitement or activity could spark off a spasm. By the time I was safely strapped in the chair, my mother was gasping for breath.

'I'll have to rest for a minute or two, Sarah, until I get my second wind. Otherwise, we'll never make it to town.'

She sat in the high-backed chair and rested her head on the winged back. Though I felt a deep surge of affection for her, at the same time I was afraid.

For a long time I'd no clear idea what an institution was, but the tone of voice my parents used when saying the word convinced me that it was no place to be. My vague fears were reinforced when Father read Oliver Twist. An institution meant cruelty and hardship. I slept badly for several nights and Mother insisted it was the story having an adverse effect on me. Now those fears suddenly came back. What will happen to me when Mother dies? Who will look after me then?

The moment my wheelchair passed through the back gate, I was overwhelmed. There was so much to see and I desperately wanted to absorb everything to savour later when I was back in the confines of home. I missed many things as my mother briskly pushed the chair down the street but each new impression brought delight.

A young mother passed us, pushing a high pram carrying a baby. The parallel reminded me of my dependency on the woman pushing my heavy wheelchair. The baby would grow up to be independent while outwardly I would remain an adult trapped in an infant's world.

'This is Castleford, Sarah,' Mother said breathlessly. 'This is where all the shops are.'

The noises I usually make when excited startled passers-by. They glanced at me furtively then hurried on, embarassed. Only the sharp clack of my mother's tongue against her teeth told me she was angry.

I was enthralled by the shop window displays; by the wonderful dresses hanging on glassy-eyed models which looked almost human. Lovely dresses with frills and flounces, in bright cheerful floral designs; a far cry from the serviceable clothes Mother made for me.

The strong aroma of herbs, spices and freshly ground coffee drifted on the air as we came to a shop called Redmans. The window was packed with flat boxes containing dried apricots, apple rings and prunes alongside boxes of dried beans. I will never forget the picture that display created or the glorious combination of fragrant smells.

When we stopped outside the greengrocer's shop I thought I was dreaming. I could never have imagined such a sight. On the pavement, arranged in tiers, were enormous mounds of shiny red and green apples set next to heaps of bright oranges. Luscious black grapes were arranged alternately with bunches of crisp green grapes along a bar in the window. Cauliflowers with firm white centres framed by crisp green leaves were like rows of giant daisies.

I wanted to reach out and touch them all; bury my face in them and breathe in their sweet tangy perfume. When Mother turned my chair away from that delightful scene, I tried to appeal to her to stay a little longer.

'We must go now, dear,' she said, turning the unwieldy chair and ignoring inquisitive stares. 'There's just one little job to do, Sarah, and then I'll take you for a walk in the Valley Gardens as a special treat.'

For the moment, Mother had just one thing on her mind. That was to get to the jeweller's shop. She said she had an unpleasant task to perform and would be glad to get it over and done with.

The jeweller's shop on the other side of the town had three brass balls hanging above the door. I wondered why they were there but my curiosity was denied me. Mother heaved my chair over the step and into the dingy shop.

'I can't risk leaving her outside,' she told the short, grey haired man who was standing behind the counter looking surprised. When my eyes became accustomed to the gloom after the bright sunlight outside, I saw that the shop was filled with treasures. The glass case beneath the counter was full of clocks and watches on the bottom shelf and above them a display of rings, earrings and brooches. The rings nestled individually in small slots in a black velvet pad, their precious stones enhanced by the reflected lights concealed inside the cabinet.

Mother handed over a small parcel and the man opened it with care. He examined the gold watch and chain and smiled. He stroked the watch face lovingly.

'It's a fine piece. A fine piece,' he repeated quietly. Then he scrutinised it closely through an eye glass.

'I think we can do business here,' he said looking at my mother, his face still contorted to keep the eye glass in place.

'I imagine you're sorry to have to part with it.'

'It has great sentimental value. It belonged to my husband, but we have no son to pass it on to and the money can be put to good use.'

I felt a deep sense of guilt. No son to pass it on to. If I hadn't been born like this there might have been brothers and sisters.

My mother drew in her breath as the jeweller offered a price for the watch. The amount took her by surprise. She calmly accepted his offer and when he handed her the huge white bank notes she folded them carefully and put them in the back compartment of her black purse. Then she tucked the purse in the bottom of her handbag.

'Whatever happens, Sarah, we musn't lose that,' she said in a whisper. Then she wiped my face and replaced my soggy scarf with a fresh dry one she'd tucked behind my chair cushion. 'And now for that special treat.'

Five minutes walk brought us to some huge wrought iron gates. They stood open, and as we passed through it was like entering a wonderland. Valley Park was ablaze with colour, each flowerbed seeming to surpass the last as Mother pushed my chair along the meandering concrete paths. I was overwhelmed by the beauty of the flowers. Red roses and pink geraniums, huge velvet pansies which were a riot of purples, blues and golds — reminding me of the exotic butterflies in the nature book Father bought me.

Mother took me twice round the small park then made for the wooden bench seat, set back from the path which bordered a magnificent rose garden. She pulled my chair to a halt and put on the brake.

'I think we deserve a little rest after all that excitement, Sarah dear,' she said, gently pushing a stray curl from my face. 'It's been quite a day for you so let's rest here a while and enjoy the lovely view, shall we?'

We sat in silence, intoxicated by the heady perfume of the roses. My love for her was overwhelming. Today my mother had given me the greatest gift of all — freedom.

The Love Of Minor Poets

Brian Lewis

When Gerry learned that Craig Raine had written a poem
after looking up his own arse with a mirror, he knew that
he had found a poet to whom he could relate. Poetry for
him, at this stage, consisted of women and men con-
templating themselves in just such a way. And here was
a major poet, someone who could easily become a Poet
Laureate, confirming this viewpoint.

Call it prejudice if you like but if your first wife spent
most of her waking hours of those final six months writing
free verse in denunciation of men in general and one in
particular, then your perspective might well be distorted.
It was only when he learned that people supplemented
their income by this activity that he sat up, took notice and
had a conversion not dissimilar to that experienced by Saul
on the road to Damascus. He began to produce poetry.

In the late seventies, the Tuesday Guardian was filled
with several column inches urging published poets to apply
for writerships-in-residence at comprehensives in places
like Sutton-in-Ashfield or Swinton, South Yorkshire. But
as the years wore on, this form of advertising got less and
less.

It was a pity, because many hours in that increasingly
depressing decade had been spent in trying to secure a
foothold — or perhaps in this case a feet hold — in the
amazing world of poetry. It had not been easy, but ten years
in the game — let us for convenience call it a game — he
had a slim volume to his credit and a curriculum vitae
which showed that he had been published by *Krux, Frax,
Wharfes and Strays,* the *Otley to Harrogate Garland* and in an
Arvon Anthology.

What he had not done, however, was to secure one of the coveted residencies. To lead fashion was his cross, or so he told everyone who would listen. 'When they wanted performance, I was into haiku modulation, when they reached there, I had moved to the iambics of heavy metal.'

Of course, this wasn't the reason he never got an interview; he didn't get one because in his first letter to the Regional Arts Association he made a faux pas. Wishing to commend his work to Richard Chambers, the Literature Officer, he had described himself as a 'peot' and asked if someone would 'cast a critical eye over his peoms.' It was generally thought that if he could not spell, he could not be serious.

Yet, had anyone bothered to look carefully at his experience, they would have recognised that apart from one absent characteristic, that of eccentricity, he was the ideal writer-in-residence. The type of writer needed for this type of work had to have suffered, be born into the working class and know first hand the mixture of greed and guile which allows writers to survive in a starkly competitive world. Jane Austen would not have been very good at the job.

When it comes to writing though, it is the eccentricity which counts. You must not only be, but also be seen to be.

Gerry's trouble was that he was not seen to be eccentric. The eccentricities in his writing models were quite revolutionary but they went unacknowledged because what interviewers (who barely looked at his verse) wanted was peculiar behaviour. Gerry was so very, very straight.

'Are you a bugger?'

'Well, no.'

'A drunk?'

'I drink a little table wine.'

'Women, do you like very young women?'

'I've been married.'

'If you saw someone about to piss on an electric fire, what would you do?'

The panel was made up of librarians who like the idea of living precariously — the Literature Officer, the three drunken writers who always had time to interview if there were expenses, and a make-weight woman.

'I'm sorry, Gerry, you got really close that time. Will you come in, Stephie and tell us — if we offer you the job, would you accept?' Everyone noticed how, with the lightest of touches, the Literature Officer nursed the slim waist through the Conference Room.

Rumour had it that Gerry got the two weeks residency with the Horbury Writers' Circle because the Literature Officer threw a piece of crusty office repartee across his shoulder as he departed towards the Pizza Hut. When confronted with imponderables, he and the secretary, in recognition of the almost daily pleas for help which came their way, used to say 'Give it to Gerry.' Gerry got the job because the secretary had changed desks and an officious temp was establishing her space and authority.

Horbury Writers' Circle was more discrete in its literary ambitions than most creative writing groups. It met 'to celebrate in verse, strict metre or free; in prose or dramatic composition, the culture of the townships of Horbury and Ossett.'

What this meant in reality was that those men and women who met weekly to read aloud thinly veiled autobiography set the scene of their unhappiness in ten square miles to the west of Wakefield City. *Lines on Horbury Bridge*, *The Road to Huddersfield*, *Where Slazenger Made Racquets* and *Mi Bretton Lass* — were the fairly typical titles for their composition; as were *Unhappiness*, *Chipped Marriage*, *Loneliness of the Soul* and *God Help Us*.

It is said that when Leavis first came north to lecture at York University, the undergraduates queued to hear him; that twenty people came to the second lecture and that by the third week he had pinned a note on his door saying — *Why not call in and have a sherry?*

Gerry's experience was not so different. The first time he saw the group, all twelve members turned up, but by the third week, only Angela and Hubert were there.

'It'll be the weather, mester. There's been gale warnings to shipping in coastal stations. Do you mind if I go too, I've got to tie down the greenhouse?'

That left Angela.

But it wasn't the weather — it was his enthusiasm which had alienated almost everyone. When he'd arrived, they'd said, 'Here's a published poet, someone who could say how it was done. Let him teach us the way.'

That is why they had pushed poetry into his hand with, 'Well is it good?' by which they meant 'is it publishable' and 'Please tell us what you think,' meaning 'tell us you like it.'

Only the very blunt, in a county renowned for its bluntness said, 'If that little bugger can get on Channel 4 and can make good money by talking to us, how come I cannot get this lot — something that speaks clearly to all classes — into print? So don't just stand there saying *Very interesting*, you patronising bastard — say how it's done.'

Of course, Gerry couldn't because when it comes down to it, there are no standards beyond the publisher's pocket. Poems which shuffle from hand to hand might be messages from a Muse but books of poems are commodities — 'Fancy a hamburger, Sheila? Fancy a poetry book, Miranda?' — and even if he could say something relevant, that really wasn't his job. His task was to enthuse an audience by reading them what he had written and at the same time introduce them to poets of the past who, in a century's time, he would snuggle up to in some Elysian Field.

Years later, when they were living out of season on the caravan park in Primrose Valley and had time to go over the events of that afternoon, she would say he knew exactly what he was doing or how else could he persuade a young mother with prospects and computer skills, to leave everything and follow his star?

She was right. To some extent Gerry was aware of the potential in the situation because when Hubert left for his allotment, he fed notes of *William Blake's Jerusalem* and *Thoughts on Todmorden* down the pack and brought forth a lecture entitled *What To Do Next*.

The wind and rain on the windows always heightened his sexuality, and in any case, he usually got an erection when reading almost anyone other than Milton and Sylvia Plath, so it did not surprise him to see that he was looking on Angela in a new way.

To his Coy Mistress by Andrew Marvell. He spoke the lines from memory, although the poem, in an alternative seventeenth century spelling, lay open on the teacher's desk.

> *Had we but world enough and time*
> *This coyness laddy were no crime.*

She raised one finger in an elegant gesture as if to say, 'Somebody up there is listening,' before contributing, 'Excuse me, Mr Morse, shouldn't it be 'lady.' *This coyness 'lady' were no crime?'*

As the teacher, he looked over his glasses without a twinkle of doubt. 'I think 'laddy' is allowable. You must remember their sexual mores are not ours and the reader of today should be expected to intervene when appropriate. I think we could also allow 'congress.' *This congress laddy were no crime.'*

She persisted. 'But surely you cannot take a line out of context and extrude it beyond common sense.'

'But why not? That is the quintessence of all criticism.'

He spoke with authority and since he knew more about poetry that she did, her finger crooked and knotted itself deeply into her ethnic necklace. It did not emerge again until half way through the explanation about 'vegetable love' when she felt a desire to clean her glasses. She took them off and wiped them with a tissue.

'You will see, I am sure, that the vegetable which grows is his penis. It is a metaphor. And since *West India Ganges side* comes immediately before that metaphor we can see that the fruit eluded to is the banana: a West Indian cash crop. It says *Our vegetable love will etc.* — so neither must we exclude the female genitalia from our equation.'

His knowledge of the clitoris came from soft porn magazines purchased at W.H. Smiths and smuggled out in the folds of the Craven Herald. His flawed knowledge of world geography was produced at a secondary school which for four consecutive years taught a course called *Where I live* but the interpretation of the removal of the glasses came from somewhere altogether more exotic.

The action of removing glasses immediately prior to sexual encounter came from the Hollywood of the thirties. When James Stewart noticed Edward G. Robinson's stenographer — the young Bette Davis — he removed her spectacles, ruffled her hair and murmured 'Now, how about that?' Lacking panache but witnessing approximately the same phenomena, Gerry Morse could only say, 'You know, Mrs Wainwright, you bear a remarkable resemblance to the young Jane Fonda.'

Finish this tale as you will. Those who see literature as reality will quickly have them coupling on the floor and among the toffee papers and torn hymn books, consummating their, let's not call it *love,* let's call it *need.* The more romantic or timorous will let them neck in the walk-in store cupboards; while those of a moral frame of mind will have her rising rapidly, saying a few words on AIDS before reporting him to the Centre Head for sexual harassment.

I know what happened and you do not. Therefore you are at liberty if you feel inclined, to invent; to bridge the gap between a classroom in Horbury Middle and temporary housing on the East Coast. Literature can do that, because, as I'm sure you will agree — invention is its justification, not publication.

Old Dog

Eileen Shaw

She points one toe on the end of a sappy leg, looking down at the instructions.

'Why'd they have those dresses up at the back like that? That bit of net, white and stiff, framing the harmless bum. Wishing for a smile. When a child, she'd smile and clap her hands for me, but this is serious, glum. Swivelling on women's hips at eight years old. Robbed. I've been robbed of her already.'

'Eurgh, Grandad, you smell of beer!'

Each loss, each withdrawal — a pain in the guts. Shouldn't care at this stage. She's the last one who will care for you, not many ever did. Just one and that not human.

Where are you going to go with your suitcase full of self-pity? You're land-locked, here in this house with its dancing shields on the walls and its plains and plaids in modern brown. Carpet the colour of dog shit. Reminds him . . .

The carriage clock ticking, ticking, mocking. Shouldn't have had that last half.

'Here y'are Dad.'

A rare cup of tea from his daughter Beth. A real man fathers girls, in some sort of twist to the normal. Any old bastard can have a son. A good woman, his daughter. They're all for doing the right thing. Get you to the Day Centre twice a week where they give you lino shapes to cut. Talks about the war and searches the faces. Talks about getting them to the polling booth. But the women are permed in their Housing Association flats and the men have lost their marbles. They smell of their jumble-sale lives and Sunday with the grandkids — most of them.

He's making a pair of slippers for Penelope who now

turns her little bum-ruff towards him and raises one slow, sappy leg, wobbling and bobbling.

'Wouldn't hurt you to say thank you, would it?'

Beth's round face with its sharp nose, like her mother's. Raised brows in a face all points and corners. Her mother was the first heart-break in a dark cinema. Seeing the wet on her lower lip as she tensed her profile, he leans forward. Sees past Mae West tipping the wink. Sees the soft reflection on that lower lip, the wetness squeezing up his heart. Then it's the whole rigmarole. For two and a half moments of pain and sickness known as love.

'Lift your legs, Dad.'

The moan of the vacuum cleaner. He was nearly asleep but she chases him with the dust.

'Dad, go lie in your room if you're going to sleep.'

'I'm watching our Penny.'

'Penny'll have to get her tea. I told you not to get changed yet!'

'I've got to practice!' Everything's a tragedy, stamping her foot. 'Miss Pascoe said I had to!'

The shrill little drawl, the glum little face under its heavy blonde fringe. Gets all this from her Dad.

He's tired, the old dog. Passing a hand in front of his face. Only way to survive. Ignore it all.

When they've gone to Penny's class, he lifts himself out of the chair and finds the kitchen like an operating theatre. Pokes about among the green peppers and the yoghurt cartons. She won't buy kippers because they're dyed, she says. Dyed. Eggs then. His fingers fumble at the plastic holder. The egg slips and slides against his palm; one out, two out. Make myself a fried mess. Can't do with her little fish dinner, her little kidney pies.

Mags used to give him plates this wide. Steaming heaps of potato, chunks of steak with gravy all over it. Rivers of gravy flowing down the mountains of mashed swede, cabbage, carrots. All with taste. All smelling of root and earth.

'Or is it me? All I can smell is packets, plastic, cellophane, cartons of carboard. Everything washed and the flavour lobotomised. There was once a dinner, on demob day . . .'

One on the floor. He laughs. It skated down his trouser leg. It splashed its thin shell onto his shoe and swam off across the crazy paving. He gets the cloth from under the sink. She has a particular one for each job — is this the right one? One for spills, one for mud, one for God knows what. Wets it. Hang on, frying pan's smoking, take if off the watchermacallit. Hob she calls it. Used to be gas. Now you don't see a naked flame. Don't see a naked anything. Cloth smarms against the yellow heart.

'One on the floor,' he mutters.

Down on his cracked knees. Feels the wet through his trouser leg, icy cold on the bare bone. Get back up then, old sod. Sling the cloth back in the cupboard. The oil crackles as he empties his eggs — smarting at the flash of them against his fingers.

He shovels it in with no-one to watch. Time was you wouldn't ask a man to 'mind his manners.' Ask him 'not to smack his lips, dip his bread in the gravy.' Ask him 'to treat eating as a pastime, a skill to be learned by the bairn' — not a pleasurable means of survival.

Kettle on. Going in his pocket for a Woodbine before he remembers.

'If you're going to smoke, Dad, you'll have to do it in your room.'

The house listens as he goes through its cool silence. Everything waiting for mistakes.

Forgetting, he lifts his legs, hums a tune he can't get the words of until it's just a sound, surrounding him. He walks, unviolated by the silence, cocooned by his voice. It's a hymn from the days of the Chapel circuit, back when he was chirpy and twanging the lasses' elastic. In love with Reenie

Sanderson, first week out of his Rotary Camp boots. The tune bringing back fat Reenie's nose against his cheek and the grass rough and springy for purchase.

The donated room with its last post comforts. The radio, the ash tray, the top window open. Coughing fit to bust. A Woodbine on, the Chapel tune turns into Lili Marlene, a natural progression. He's back in the Phoney War with Mags on the roof, fire-watching for the sewing machine factory where she worked. She wrote to him in Burma, they used to say, torch letters.

'Oggy's gorra torch,' they'd say, 'lucky bleeder.'

If it wasn't for the war he'd never have gone further than the Isle of Wight. No need, he'd say, not liking the idea of foreigners.

Takes his Woodbine back down the stairs. Pours his tea, thick and orange, like she never does. In the hall he tugs his forelock to Chas and Di on the wall. Used to be able to fart to order. Got the wind sucked out of him. Still, the women like to keep their icons polished.

That was it, when Trudy had pups behind the back of the sofa. Soft round eyes pleading and out they eased in their bruised sacs. He watched as she cleaned them. A cross-labrador, Trudy. Best friend ever.

'We'd no room and no-one wanted dogs just after the war. Mags held Trudy's head so she couldn't see what I was up to. The soft part of the bone on the back of the head. Each one. She only had four the first time. The second lot we got rid of to a pet shop. No better end, I expect. Those days it was known. But Trudy so proud and her tongue going over with infinite care. Moments you look on, you shudder now. You can't see how it was done. Soft beggar, my Dad would've said. Not over Trudy, though. Loved me, that dog, which is more than you can say.'

'Ah, but I lost them all. Lost Mags over the white-limbed woman at the Town Hall where I was a porter. And then Beth comes along the years. Sniffing me out. I say, 'What happened to Trudy?' and she's upset because I don't ask for her Mam.'

'I knew she'd gone. Someone told me in the Scarborough Taps. I sent white lilies. Her favourite. Cancer, the bloke said. Beth tells me the old dog got out and went on the railway line. Somebody came to bring back her collar, Beth says, 'I was alone, in the house. Can you imagine how I felt?' She looks at me, asking for sympathy. 'A little girl I was, ten years old.' Accusing me of not being there.'

Aye well, he's here now.

Going back to his place as a fire-iron. Runs the tap on the tab. Collects his ash in a dishcloth. Looks down at himself. Diminished. Stomach like Trudy's in whelp. Just bones for the rest of him. And egg all down his trousers.

He takes a slice of bread and jam with him, but lately he feels he can't swallow everything. The shelf of his upper throat holds the food as if it has forgotten the necessary convulsions. His body poises, and then it's over. The old messages get through. His oesophagus remembers that neat trick of the sinews. But soon he'll be afraid to put food in his mouth. If his mind forgets and his body takes over.

'Where there's life,' he reminds himself.

His doctor looks like Emile Savundra, he told Beth.

She said, 'Who?'

She's no time for the past any more.

Her husband Bri doesn't know either, doesn't want to know. Only things he knows he reads in The Sun.

Old dog reads them all. Public Lending Library, nine-fifteen a.m. one day behind. For a minute the transcripts of high windows, bright air, the echo of the parquet and the dry, urgent smell of books. Paper dust compacting into bone-crunching sneezes that throw his head from his body on an elastic neck, bouncing round the room.

He touches a finger to the cold crepe of skin over his upper sinuses, feels the fluid shift in repose. Lapses into the slackness that passes for sleep.

Later, the February afternoon is like bow-gut, taut across the shimmering sky. He guesses rain, after an hour of threat from the wind. Remembers: Saturday.

He'll go out. Walk round the market. A couple of halves at the George. Bri's at the match. Spends the morning visiting his mother, and then the game. They're going up to the First Division and Bri's elated.

'Think of it Dad, eh? Fuckin' Liverpool eh? Fuckin' Liverpool!!'

Away from his wife, Bri grows two feet taller, his face animates with separation, giving natural expression release. Didn't he do the same, once? A man's enthusiasm, after all. A man's passions.

Clearing phlegm in the bathroom, he sees what might be blood among the jelly, dismisses it. Not ready for the hospital bed, Beth trying to be cheerful, talking about the other patients and what's been on the telly. Please Christ, no.

The threatening wind has eased as he pulls his scarf up round his ears. The stupor from the dinner hour lifts like fog as the cold smacks his face, and he grins.

Notes the thin garden she expects him to tend since Bri has no interest. He's put in daffs. Easy, and should please her need for respectable, orderly colour. Like mother, like daughter, confuses him. So much the same with them, but the idea's sold short.

Mags never had her windows clean enough. Meekness and superstition. Sewing dresses to the big band on the wireless, shirts to Workers' Playtime. Afraid of electricity. Afraid of the dark. Aye, afraid of him.

Never could stand to hear a woman cry.

Something turns him away from the town and up the rise of terraced houses where he used to go with Trudy. Mags too sometimes, when she took time off from the neat and the clean. Somewhere along these streets is the house they rented after the war. His eyes dust mildly along the new paint and re-pointed brickwork.

Blue velvet curtains, she wants. Three months she works in the fish shop for them. She wants him to take the same pleasure; guilt fingers his guts. He's doing ten hour shifts, wants his pint and a warm bed.

Another ghost leering in the lumber room of memories. Feeling inside for the slump, the whimper of self, striving for comfort with legs, arms and genitals.

'I had no choice. The bottle-blonde wanted it up her every night. The fever wheezed along my veins. And she had such touches; a purple silver bedstead, candles on the mantle, sticky French scent, white parted limbs, loose red tongue curling in my head, she's aching in my body like an ancient illness.'

He went looking for the same secrets in another place. Spent years going after them between the work. Always another place, and the whores get younger. Comfort gone for the itch and scratch of sex.

Breaching the hill, his breath rasping, he feels tears form, anger like a cloud in his breast, pushing against the rapid heartbeat. Spits a white flag on the ground and steps on it, dark disgust treading down the threads of his disease. The same love and regret is vinegar, not wine. No more wine, old dog.

He sits. Jolts down on the ground, a collapsed marionette, grit biting his arse, then jerks back to lie on the grass in some parody of relief. His stubborn legs have fire in their joints. Pain burns in the groin as lush and potent as lust.

The stiff grass is searing his hands, the rumbling sky is chasing him across the hills. Wind and breath in the clogged outlets of nose and mouth, entering the chambers of his body. Cleaning him, clearing him, absolving him in his infirmity.

Lie here a while, always wanting more than you can have. You can't get up on the old moor nowadays. Can't have the old dog fetching sticks. Can't follow the scent, or even smell it now. Old dog's dead, travelled too far.

Now the framework trembles at the stew of gas and chemicals. Thin pipes and blocked channels, churning in its bag of skin. The brain porous and pitted as a stiff-soaped sponge; feeling around it for remnants, torn curtains, blanched by too much sun, too much rain.

In a minute he'll get up. Bri will be back, checking his pools. Beth in the kitchen touting up another dainty tea. Penny scowling because she can't get up on her points. This is what he gets even if they don't love him, but feels duty like a turd, easing out.

There's no rest, is there? For the wicked.

Voice Boxes

Karen White

Kevin Shipside was being beaten half to death. Body and soul, he was hurled over the angled desk till he came eye to eye with the hole in his inkwell. Miss O'Brien told him he deserved the cat-o'-nine-tails and said what a lucky boy he was, to feel only her hands cutting across his spindly legs. The rest of us sat rigid, hearts throbbing furiously as the cracks whipped across Kevin's calves.

He screamed and tears erupted from his puckered eyes.

'No Miss. It wasn't me Miss. Honest Miss . . .'

'You were seen, Kevin Shipside,' she panted. 'I'll teach you to throw stones at Father Peters in the presbytery garden while he's saying his office.'

Crack! Another slap left its mark on the back of Kevin's legs. A shuffled chair and a nervous voice interrupted the punishment.

'Please Miss, it wasn't Kevin it was me.'

All eyes turned to the trembling, red faced confessor, Trevor Shipside — Kevin's twin brother. The abrupt halt in mid-slap drained the colour from Miss O'Brien's cheeks. Beads of powder-stained sweat dripped from her nose.

Kevin did not go uncompensated however. For this error of judgement, he was awarded not just one, but a whole bag of Miss O'Brien's precious jelly babies. Then she turned to Trevor.

'P-p-please Miss. I didn't know Father Peters was the other side of the wall,' he pleaded, 'I was just trying to knock some apples off the apple tree. When Father Peters climbs up his ladder with a bucket of apples, to throw at us in the playground, I can never catch any — and I didn't think he'd mind me just having one.'

'So you thought you'd steal one did you? For that you deserve an extra slap! I don't know why I don't give you the cat-o'-nine-tails, Trevor Shipside. Stealing apples from the presbytery garden indeed. They're private apples. Look what happened in the Garden of Eden. If Adam and Eve had left the apple tree alone, you wouldn't be leaning over this desk right now.'

The thrashing commenced. Miss O'Brien charged like a bull. Trevor vibrated on the desk, scattering his pencil and jotter in different directions.

'Never forget it was Adam and Eve who brought pain and suffering into the world through the first sin. Which was what, Trevor Shipside?'

'Scrumping Miss.'

'It was disobedience you stupid boy! Dis-o-bedience.'

Punishment over, she retired breathless, behind the piano. Taking out her powder compact she daubed her face with orange powder. Tacky pink lipstick was drawn around the rim of her gaping mouth. After an inspection of her teeth and tongue, she sent an explosive blow into her handkerchief, and once the contents had been examined, tucked the snotty article up her sleeve.

She spread out her music sheets; then prodded her butterfly glasses onto the bridge of her nose with her left index finger, while her other hand re-adjusted her enormous bosom, so that it didn't collide with her frenzied hands shooting across the keyboard.

'I hope your voice boxes are open this morning,' she boomed, playing the opening notes of When Irish Eyes Are Smiling.

Kevin's and Trevor's sobs were drowned as she hit the piano keys in a fury, shouting that she couldn't hear us because our voice boxes were closed!

Fingering my throat, I was unable to feel any square object in there — just a round lumpy bit. I had a deformity and I was terrified she'd spot it!

162

'And look happy, smile . . . When Irish eyes are smiling.'
As she sang she stretched her neck upwards displaying her
lumpy bit. It seemed that Miss O'Brien didn't have a square
voice box either, so I decided a voice box was like a soul,
there but invisible.

When our voices were open and in good working order,
she let us sing Wooden Heart by Elvis 'the pelvis' Presley.
On bad days when we didn't hit the right notes, it was Latin
hymns.

We didn't need amplifiers. Sea shanties, songs of dear
old Ireland, My *Body* Lies Over the Ocean — and Latin
hymns, echoed off the high distempered walls unaided.
Miss O'Brien's favourite was Tantum Ergo, which caused
her mouth to open like a tunnel, and her lips to project
like a tube. As I sang *Tandem* Ergo, I tried not to think of
bicycles made for two.

This particular day, however, voice boxes were on their
best behaviour, and as a special treat we learnt the words
of a new song. On the cover of the music sheet it said
Bachelor Boy by Cliff Richard. Trevor and Kevin had
stopped crying and sang out with the rest of us . . . 'I'll
be a bachelor boy until my dying day . . .' Miss O'Brien
was obsessed with celibacy and death.

Dad had also taken to singing that song, ever since he'd
heard it on Two Way Family Favourites. I expect it was
because he worked at Batchelors food factory, operating the
magic eye that sorted out the bad peas. He brought home
lots of packets of rejects which he said had fallen off the
conveyor belt the wrong way.

Reject stew was my favourite and Mam said it helped to
eke out his slave wages so we didn't need to get so many
things on tick anymore. But for a few weeks reject stew was
the only thing we ate when Dad had to go into hospital
to have his tonsils out.

'Has his voice box come loose?' I asked.

'What?' said Mam, not understanding my question.

Instead of Dad's voice yelling — 'What the bloody hell do you call this? Looks like a bloody pig hole' — as he kicked the cluttered chaos across the yard, and my tricycle into the lav door, the only thing that wafted down the outside passage was the smell of reject pies and peas. The house was too quiet.

I was regularly handed an armful of empties to return for a few coppers to pay the tallyman. Clanking my empties in the string bag along Shaw Street to the off-licence was a serious responsibility. Its thick panelled door had a gleaming brass latch and a smoked glass window, with swirling scrolls and J. WOODS HOME ALES engraved in bold letters.

Inside, the little room glowed with Jim's polished trophies. My nose rested on the wooden hatch and my eyes scanned the shields and silver cups. There was a huge green monster in a glass cabinet. Its skin was as shiny as Jim's trophies and its teeth as mean as Miss O'Brien's.

'I do like your crocodile Mr Woods. Did you bring it back from Africa?' I plucked up courage to ask, one day.

Jim laughed as he tightly screwed down the black spiral tops on the empties.

'Crocodile? Africa? Nay I caught that o'er at Sandhill Lake. That there's a pike fish — look there's its fins. And that's the cup I won for catching him,' he nodded and pointed.

'I never knew fish had teeth, Mr Woods.'

'Teeth? Pike'll bite right through the net if you're not careful, not to mention eating young ducks.'

Jim gave me ninepence and a pat on the head but somehow, visiting the off-licence wasn't the same after that. In my imagination I'd seen Jim wrestling with a crocodile, like Tarzan on the Saturday morning pictures.

Five o'clock Friday, the insurance man was due. After slipping the last few shillings into the meter, me and Mam hid behind the sofa, leaving the reject stew to simmer on the gas. It burned because he was late coming.

A few days later she caught word that a local farm was looking for women to pea pull. So she became part of a gang journeying by tractor-trailer to Thorpe Salvin and some days I went with her, playing between the rows and furrows while she picked and pulled. Her earnings improved in my absence which enabled her to fill more bags.

During a tea break, one of the lasses gave her a do-it-yourself magazine, full of glossy pages of manicured models transforming old fashioned furniture for only ten and sixpence! So that week, through keeping up the supply of peas for Batchelors, she was able to buy a new piece of oilcloth for the doorway, a pot of brilliant primrose paint to adorn the utility furniture, and a saw to mutilate their old wooden bed. Dad wasn't half going to be surprised when he came out of hospital!

With turbanned head and grubby face, she manhandled the bed and amputated its legs to create an instant Deluxe Divan. Chairs were stood on pages of the Daily Herald while a coat of brilliant primrose was applied.

Eventually, tired and weary, but with a satisfied smile, she punched the paint brushes up and down in a jam jar of turps while I warmed my pyjamas by the fire.

'Can I sleep in the new bed with you tonight?' I asked.

'Only if you don't fidget.'

I promised I wouldn't, even though I could already feel the excitement welling up. I ran up the stairs like a clog hopping elephant — as Dad used to say before we got a stair carpet — and dived into bed. But now I could no longer run my fingers over the carved love birds on the bed head and I felt quite sorry that they were outside by the bin.

When Mam came to bed she tucked a pillow between us in case I fidgeted. Just as we were drifting off, with the smell of paint to remind us of the miracles that could be achieved with back-breaking work and ten and sixpence, the new Deluxe Divan did the splits and collapsed around us! In her ambition for modern design, Mam had sawn away the bed's vital supports. We slept among the wreckage, too tired to care.

When Dad first came out of hospital, he didn't rant and shout like he usually did when things got into a mess, so I guessed his voice box still wasn't working right. He made up for it though when his speech returned.

'Things have gone to the dogs,' was the first thing he said. 'And that's where I'm going.'

He took up his donkey jacket, wound one of my Mam's scarves round his neck, popped a couple of shillings that were meant for the meter in his pocket, and went down to the Town Ground to watch the whippet racing.

He reappeared well after closing time and clumped up to bed singing 'A four legged friend, he'll never let you down . . .'

But it did.

Jack Parker And The Graduate

Michael Yates

Jack Parker tore off two folios of copy paper, folded a carbon inside, and rolled the resulting sandwich into his typewriter. It stuck, and the paper crumpled and tore. 'Fuck,' said Jack.

It wasn't the most dignified thing for a forty-four-year-old senior reporter on a long-established Yorkshire evening newspaper to say to his typewriter. It wasn't even his typewriter, just the one he'd managed to lift from young Mayhew's desk. This business about typewriters was a pain, but complaining got you nowhere. Blame the recession. Blame the fact that an average of four thousand and eighty-seven fewer punters bought the Castlefield Echo last year than the year before.

'Sorry, Jack . . .' said Peter Cronin, the news editor, when he'd gone through the ritual.

Peter had once been a junior reporter alongside Jack. Amazingly, (because Jack knew his appetite for Italian food) he still retained his slim build in contrast to Jack's thickening middle. And the last five years had seen a deepening of his natural tan, the result of Aegean fortnights and sessions at the Castlefield Solarium, beside which, Jack's pale, lounge bar complexion provided a doughy comparison.

'Sorry, Jack. I know it's a bugger — but it's the same for everyone. Only the copytakers and Phyllis get their own personal typewriter. Money's tighter than a canary's bum right now.'

'But Phyllis doesn't need one,' said Jack, referring to the slim cheerful brunette in large brass earrings, whose official title was newsdesk secretary. 'All she does is make lists.'

Cronin sighed and pushed his goldrimmed glasses up

another notch on his handsome aquiline nose — now beginning to show, to Jack's shrewd eye — a network of tiny red veins through that tan.

'I sympathise, Jack, believe me. But it's company rules, old son. Break the rules for one and we'd have to do it for everybody.' He spread his hands in a gesture of resignation then ran the left one through his blow wave — prematurely flecked with grey, Jack noticed. 'Blame the boss. Blame Amalgamated Newspapers. Go and see Hailey if you're really bothered.'

But Jack had made his point. He knew a talk with Hailey the editor would be as useful as a cup of warm spit. He glanced across to the dozen or so reporters' desks shoved together in units of four along the outer wall, where bright-eyed boys with studs in their ears and girls with 'Say NO to rape' sewn on the pockets of their jeans wrestled with tangled telephone wires and huddled possessively over spiral-bound notebooks.

There was only one typewriter not under guard at that moment. It sat on Dick Mayhew's desk and Dick was out.

When Jack got there, he found it already contained the first folio of a story with Dick's name and the tagline BUS on it. Jack tore it out, dropped it in the bin and carried the typewriter back to his desk.

It took him three attempts to get his first folio in straight. Then he tried to adjust the margins to his own comfortable length, and the right hand margin kept springing back. He had managed to type 'J. Parker staff with pix GOLD 1' when he was made suddenly aware of Dick standing by his elbow.

Dick spoke quietly and very deliberately in that uncertain tenor voice of his so that Jack knew at once he was showing determination. 'Sorry, Jack. That's my typewriter. I need to have it back, please.' He was a tall, red-faced youth with short black hair and a trim goatee beard which only served to emphasise the baby roundness of his face. Right now that face was trying hard for an expression of firmness.

'Only the copytakers and Phyllis get their own personal typewriter,' said Jack, 'I sympathise, but it's company rules. Break the rules for one and we'd have to do it for everybody.'

Dick took four or five seconds to summon a reaction. Then he breathed hard and the redness of his cheeks increased.

'I'd already started typing,' he said, then repeated it in a lower register, 'I'd already started typing and I had to go to the bog. For God's sake, I was only away two minutes! And I'd started my first folio. You don't take away a man's typewriter when he's started his folio.'

'You know,' said Jack, 'I don't think this is your typewriter. It was pushed right in the middle of the desks. Maybe somebody else has got yours.'

'It's mine. It's got my Ian Dury sticker. And it's got a faulty right hand margin. You need to push the shift key to make it stay.'

'Ah,' said Jack. He pushed the shift key. 'Well, I didn't see any folio. Maybe you threw it away. You can do that sometimes and not remember.'

'I'm sure I didn't do that, Jack. It's my typewriter and I want it back, please.'

For a moment, Jack wondered if it was really worth it. But he'd already typed the heading on his own first folio, and to surrender now would be something of a humiliation. He decided on a reasoned approach.

'Look, son, I've got an eight par piece to do for Cronin. He needs it in five minutes. After that, the thing is yours. Eight paragraphs. Five minutes.'

He raised his right hand, a gesture of peace, and spread the fingers in a concrete image of the time required that not even Dick could fail to absorb. Then he saw Cronin had joined them.

'You two having a spot of bother?' asked Cronin.

'Mr Parker has my typewriter,' said Dick, 'and I need to

do that piece on the bus strike for city edition. I'd already started my first folio.'

'What are you doing, Jack? Anything important, old mate?' Jack sat back with a sigh, in the sure knowledge that he had lost the contest. 'That Perkins golden wedding. The retired dental technician. For tomorrow, inside page.'

'Ah,' said Cronin, employing that tone of moderation most probably favoured by Solomon in ordering the dismemberment of babies, 'Only ten minutes to deadline for city edition, and that bus strike is front page stuff. I've known you long enough to realise you won't stand on your dignity on this one, Jack.'

'You're the boss,' said Jack, and pulled GOLD 1 out of the roller, tearing the carbon right across. On the back it said Copyfilm. 'But I never saw any folio,' he added, looking hard at Dick.

'You two fancy a coffee?' said Cronin, 'I'm parched and I might as well stand the round. Sugar and milk, Dick? Milk and no sugar for you, Jack. Wise man. Deadly stuff at your age. Is the machine working today? Be right back.'

Afterwards, Jack sat staring into the plastic cup. 'You don't take a man's typewriter when he's started his folio,' he mimicked. What sort of people were they hiring these days? Pompous little asses. Graduates. Everybody these days had to be a graduate.

It hadn't been like that a quarter of a century ago when Jack first joined. It was a different breed then, local boys just out of school who knew their way around. In those days you didn't get two years of college to play newspapers — you learned by doing it, by making a fool of yourself. If you didn't ask the right question at the right time, you were sent back to ask again. And again. And again. Until you curled up inside with the shame of it. But you got it right in the end.

Jack glanced at his watch. Five to twelve. A bit early for lunch, but the golden wedding could wait. He'd been told so officially. He'd better get off before they dropped any more crap on him.

He stood in the lounge of The Greyhound, drinking Bell's whisky and water while Gerry Field sipped bitter. Gerry was a Crown Court man, one of the Echo's team of three. It meant regular hours, solid stories, few surprises at the end of the day. Which was why, by the time it was half past twelve, he could count on an adjournment and a pint and a chicken sandwich.

Gerry was twelve years older than Jack, with a mop of thick, white hair. He was already cultivating the hobbies — gardening and pottery — designed to carry him through retirement without further loss of sanity. At one time Jack had considered him a bit of a bore. For as long as Jack could remember, it seemed people had always referred to 'Old Gerry' and joked behind his back about the quaintness of style that produced intros like 'Said to have been unemployed for eighteen months and of previous good character, a Castlefield man was alleged to have attacked his thirty-five year old common-law wife with a meat cleaver.'

But Jack had recently discovered a compatibility with the older man. After all, they were both remnants of the time when Jim Corrigan had been editor, when news was news.

'It were a solid grounding then,' Gerry was saying, wiping the froth from his pepper and salt moustache, 'You came in cold and did everything. Councils, courts, inquests, fires, road traffic accidents . . .

'Talking about RTAs,' interrupted Jack, remembering a good tale that he was sure he hadn't mentioned to Gerry before, 'The second day I was here — the second day, mind you — Corrigan sent me out to pick up a picture. It was a kid called Billy Linfoot, that I'd been to school with. Got killed on his motorbike. When Corrigan heard I knew him, he said to get round — raw lad or not.

'I said who I was, Billy's friend, and I said I was with the Echo, but I don't think they took it in. His mam was crying her eyes out and the old man was stood about shellshocked, you know the way they get. I made them a cup of tea and said — did they have a picture, something to remember him by? We were both in the scouts and I ended up with one of him in uniform. Well, I had to get it back for the early edition and it was the best I could do.

'But Corrigan was pleased as punch. When he heard about the cup of tea, he bought me a pint of shandy. *Kept your head* he said *you've got what it takes.* I always remember that.'

'Couldn't get away with it these days,' said Gerry, shaking his head, 'Press Council would be on you like a ton of bricks.'

Jack laughed. 'Corrigan never had any time for the Press Council. Remember what he used to say? *Press Council? I've heard of Castlefield Borough Council, but this Press Council's a bit outside our area.* Anyway,' he added, perceiving the slight tone of reproach in Gerry's voice, 'what harm did it do? I saw they got the picture back. Want another?'

'Not for me. Back before the beak at two-fifteen.'

Jack ordered another Bell's from Colin the barman, and turned back to Gerry.

'Do you remember,' he said, 'that story I had about the alligator? That taxi driver . . . Harry something . . . big football fan. Used to see him at Bromwich Lane when I covered the matches.

'Anyway, he gets called out in the middle of the night to pick up this couple stranded on the Great North Road. When he gets there, their van's broken down and they've got this nine-month-old alligator and a sixteen-foot python, and this Harry has to . . .'

'Jack,' said Gerry, draining the glass, 'I've got to run. Sorry, but I've got to pick up some clay from the craft shop and do a spot of shopping for the wife. See you.' He turned and waved as he reached the door. 'See you don't have too much now.'

Jack nodded goodbye, then looked round the room for anyone else he might know. Disappointed, he found a seat in the corner.

His brief euphoria, talking over old times with Gerry, had suddenly dissipated. What was Gerry on about with the drinking? Was he serious? Jack had only had three. Maybe it was four. But not enough to get drunk. Not enough to even look vaguely drunk.

He took stock of himself. He was still walking straight. Not talking too loud. Talking pretty quietly with Gerry. Was his speech slurred? He had two false teeth at the front and sometimes the plate worked loose and it could, he knew, give the wrong impression . . .

He remembered now. Harry Porter. And it had been a great intro — *It's enough to make an alligator weep crocodile tears.* It made all editions with a byline and a little cartoon from the graphics department of a croc with a suitcase hitching a lift. Another pint of shandy for the lad who found the crazy stories.

You didn't need a degree to write news, and Corrigan knew it. You didn't need 'O' Level English for that matter, because real news wrote itself. *Angry mums up in arms. Petticoat pickets in down-tools drama. Two killed in road crash horror. Police today are hunting. Firebug. Massive head injuries.*

If you wrote *petticoat pickets* these days, some bright slip on the sub's table would tell you it trivialised women, and they'd rewrite it.

Corrigan knew about news. This bugger Hailey didn't. News was death and fire and rap and football, with a smattering of funnies so the punters didn't take it all too seriously.

Bitterly, Jack recalled the new catchphrases of the Hailey regime, those all-pervading slogans that had already slipped into the collective consciousness of the newsroom: in-depth, news behind the news, the information that affects people's lives.

So now it was figures, tables, graphs, rates, taxes, wage claims, councillors' expenses, comparison, analysis.

And the so-called 'investigations'. Three quarters of a page on why it took three years to build the Manx Corner flyover. Why the Town Hall renovation went two million pounds over budget. Why a hundred and eighty slabs in the New Street shopping precinct had to be replaced twenty-one months after the official opening. More figures, tables, graphs. If Hailey could calculate how many times council officials went to the lavatory against the amount of paper they used, he'd have somebody in graphics doing diagrams of their bums.

No wonder they lost readers. No wonder they couldn't afford typewriters.

What the hell did Gerry mean, *don't drink too much?* He'd only had three or four. But people could do that, get the wrong impression. Like the time . . .

Dick Mayhew would be down on him. Waiting for him to get back. Jack could imagine that whining schoolboy voice. 'Mr Parker's been gone a long time, hasn't he?' Little sneak. And then, when Jack got in, he'd be watching every move, looking for that tell-tale deliberateness, that slight exaggeration of gesture that would be taken as a giveaway. Old Parker pissed again. Like the time . . .

Two o'clock. Better get back. He drained the glass. To hell with it. He was a senior reporter. He didn't clock in like a bloody bus driver. If he took a long lunch once in a while, well, he made up for it plenty of times working late on stories. BIG stories.

He took the glass back to the bar. 'Same again, Mr Parker?' asked Colin.

'You know what?' said Jack, 'Carbon paper isn't carbon paper any more. It's Copyfilm.'

'I didn't know that, Mr Parker. See you tomorrow then.'

When he got back, he made for the coffee machine. There was a notice in biro hung from one of the knobs: THIS

MODULE IN AN ONGOING INOPERATIVE SITUA-
TION. He went back to his desk and watched himself sit
down.

'Right,' he said. He listened to the word. It sounded okay.
He looked round for his notebook — it was lying under
a copy of the early edition. He didn't bother with the paper;
there was nothing of his in today except a five par job on
he latest binmen's pay negotiations. It began *There was no
change today* . . .

He thought he saw Dick Mayhew out of the corner of
his eye staring across at him. He ignored Dick Mayhew.
He began to whistle, then stopped. The Perkins golden
wedding. Better get it done with. He thumbed through the
book until he recognised the relevant pages of spidery
shorthand.

Now, of course, he needed a typewriter. Dick Mayhew
wasn't using his. Not that it was his anyway. With an effort,
Jack got to his feet. Slow now. Careful now. In control. Like
the time . . .

He stopped. Dick was standing talking to Cronin. Suddenly he knew they were talking about *him*. He felt sick.
Like the time . . .

. . . Like the time Kidders' department store is burning
down, biggest fire in Castlefield in fifteen years, and young
Jack Parker is running news desk because Baker the old
news editor is off with the flu. Some young reporter, Ross
or Charlesworthy or Maddock, one of the good young ones
of that time who went on to the nationals, phoning in
names, addresses, ages — *Store manager denies emergency exits
closed.* And young Jack Parker putting the pieces together
coolly and calmly. Ross or Charlesworth or Maddock
checking with police and hospital, and young Jack Parker
telling the subs to 'pull the front page on the early edition,
ditch that lead about council house repairs,' and typing the
intro from Ross or Charlesworth or Maddock's copy. *Three
people are believed dead today* . . . adding new paragraphs as

they come in, and then it's gone. And young Jack Parker is organising a whole new story, an update for the late night final with pictures and eyewitnesses and Corrigan comes in, his eyes ablaze, waving the story, waving young Jack Parker's story, and shouting at young Jack Parker 'Nobody's dead! They've been accounted for! It's here in the copy! Can't you bloody read?' — and there it is, in black and white, names, injuries, condition checks, tucked away at the end. Phoned over late by Ross or Charlesworth or Maddock with a special note, unnoticed, to *please change earlier copy, three people believed dead now accounted for* and a front page pulled apart again and the whole edition late on the streets because of young Jack Parker.

And young Jack Parker trying to explain how someone young and very scared behind the confident exterior can make such a blunder, but unable to find the words and, in his sudden terror, is violently sick and Corrigan shouting: 'You're pissed! Get out of my sight! You'll never work news desk again!'

I wasn't drunk, I wasn't drunk. Not on two pints of shandy. Jack was looking up at Dick Mayhew.

'Well?' he said. He pulled himself up to his full height, which brought him level with Dick's beard. 'Well?'

'I'm sorry, Jack. I found that folio. In the bin. I must have thrown it away like you said. I just told Mr Cronin. I'm sorry I made it look . . .'

'That's okay,' said Jack, tapping his finger on Dick's chest to emphasise the point, 'We all make mistakes. To tell you the truth, I'd forgotten all about it.'